Michael Morpurgo

From Hereabout Hill

A collection of short stories

mammoth

First published in Great Britain in 2000 by Mammoth,
an imprint of Egmont Children's Books Limited
a division of Egmont Holding Limted
239 Kensington High Street, London W8 6SA

ISBN 0 7497 2872 8

10 9 8 7 6 5 4

A CIP catalogue record for this book
is available from the British Library

Printed in Great Britain by Cox & Wyman Ltd, Reading, Berkshire

Michael Morpurgo

Michael Morpurgo has written over sixty books, many short stories, screenplays, and even two musicals. His books have won the Whitbread Award (*The Wreck of the Zanzibar*), the Smarties Book Prize (*The Butterfly Lion*) and the Circle of Gold Award (*King of the Cloud Forests*), and several have been shortlisted for the Carnegie Medal. In addition, two novels have been adapted for television and film (*My Friend Walter* and *Why the Whales Came*).

Michael and his wife Clare were each awarded an MBE in the 1999 Queen's Birthday Honours list for services for youth, in recognition of their work for the charity *Farms for City Children*.

Other titles by Michael Morpurgo, published by Mammoth

An interview with Michael Morpurgo
Arthur: High King of Britain
Escape from Shangri-La
Friend or Foe
The Ghost of Grania O'Malley
Kensuke's Kingdom
King of the Cloud Forests
Little Foxes
Long Way Home
Mr Nobody's Eyes
My Friend Walter
The Nine Lives of Montezuma
Twist of Gold
Waiting for Anya
War Horse
The War of Jenkins' Ear
The White Horse of Zennor
Why the Whales Came
The Wreck of the Zanzibar

For younger readers

Colly's Barn
Conker
Jo-Jo the Melon Donkey
The Marble Crusher
The Sandman and the Turtles
Snakes and Ladders

Edited by Michael Morpurgo

Muck and Magic – Stories from the Countryside

For Miriam

Contents

From Hereabout Hill

by Seàn Rafferty

From Hereabout Hill
the sun early rising
looks over his fields
where a river runs by;
at the green of the wheat
and the green of the barley
and Candlelight Meadow
the pride of his eye.

The clock on the wall
strikes eight in the kitchen
the clock in the parlour
says twenty to nine;
the thrush has a song
and the blackbird another
the weather reporter
says cloudless and fine.

It's green by the hedge
and white by the peartree
in Hereabout village
the date is today;
it's seven by the sun
and the time is the springtime
the first of the month and
the month must be May.

Foreword

Writers and miners have something in common, I think. Daily we search for and hope to find the rich seams we need. Some writers discover a seam so productive that they simply keep digging the way the seam leads them. My problem is that I am too easily bored. I find a rich seam, dig like crazy, and then move on to a new seam, a different seam. I may return to the old one later, I often do.

This somewhat impatient and immature way of mining for my stories is reflected in this collection of tales. And there is a good reason for it, a good excuse, anyway. All of these stories, except one, have been written at the behest of someone else, a friend or an editor. So I've been digging away contentedly in my seam, when some story mining expert (editor) comes up with a proposal that I might write a short story about such and such. 'Stop your digging there,' she says. 'Look over there and follow that seam. It looks promising.' Whether I do as I'm told entirely depends upon who's doing the telling.

It was Miriam Hodgson who so often came up with proposals that I should explore new areas. That is why this book is dedicated to her – one of the truly great story mining experts. She knows where the gold runs deep and true, how a writer gets at it, and she's good on the smelting too. She likes these stories, which makes me hope and believe that you will too.

Michael Morpurgo
June 2000

PS 'From Hereabout Hill' was written by a dear friend and wonderful poet, Seàn Rafferty, who lived in a cottage on the farm until his death in 1993. The 'Hereabout Hill' he writes of was his hill and is my hill, the place I live, the place I write my stories.

The Giant's Necklace

So, a mining story to start with. For many years I used to go every summer to Zennor. I read Cornish legends, researched the often tragic history of tin mining in Penwith, wandered the wild moors above Zennor Churchtown. I wrote a book of five short stories called The White Horse of Zennor. *This is the first.*

The necklace stretched from one end of the kitchen table to the other, around the sugar bowl at the far end and back again, stopping only a few inches short of the toaster. The discovery on the beach of a length of abandoned fishing line draped with seaweed had first suggested the idea to Cherry; and every day of the holiday since then had been spent in one single-minded pursuit, the creation of a necklace of glistening pink cowrie shells. She had sworn to herself and to everyone else that the necklace would not be complete until it

3

reached the toaster; and when Cherry vowed she would do something, she invariably did it.

Cherry was the youngest in a family of older brothers, four of them, who had teased her relentlessly since the day she was born, eleven years before. She referred to them as 'the four mistakes', for it was a family joke that each son had been an attempt to produce a daughter. To their huge delight Cherry reacted passionately to any slight or insult whether intended or not. Their particular targets were her size, which was diminutive compared with theirs, and her dark flashing eyes that could wither with one scornful look, her 'zapping' look, they called it. Although the teasing was interminable it was rarely hurtful, nor was it intended to be, for her brothers adored her; and she knew it.

Cherry was poring over her necklace, still in her dressing gown. Breakfast had just been cleared away and she was alone with her mother. She fingered the shells lightly, turning them gently until the entire necklace lay flat with the rounded pink of the shells all uppermost. Then she bent down and breathed on each of them in turn, polishing them carefully with a napkin.

'There's still the sea in them,' she said to no one in particular. 'You can still smell it, and I washed them and washed them, you know.'

'You've only got today, Cherry,' said her mother coming over to the table and putting an arm round her. 'Just today, that's all. We're off back home tomorrow morning first thing. Why don't you call it a day, dear? You've been at it every day – you *must* be tired of it by now. There's no need to go on, you know. We all think it's a fine necklace and quite long enough. It's long enough surely?'

Cherry shook her head slowly. 'No,' she said. 'Only that little bit left to do and then it'll be finished.'

'But they'll take hours to collect, dear,' her mother said weakly, recognising and at the same time respecting her daughter's persistence.

'Only a few hours,' said Cherry, bending over, her brows furrowing critically as she inspected a flaw in one of her shells, 'that's all it'll take. D'you know, there are five thousand, three hundred and twenty-five shells in my necklace already? I counted them, so I know.'

'Isn't that enough, Cherry?' her mother said desperately.

'No,' said Cherry. 'I said I'd reach the toaster, and I'm going to reach the toaster.'

Her mother turned away to continue the drying-up.

'Well, I can't spend all day on the beach today, Cherry,' she said. 'If you haven't finished by the time we come away, I'll have to leave you there. We've got to pack up and tidy the house – there'll be no time in the morning.'

'I'll be all right,' said Cherry, cocking her head on one side to view the necklace from a different angle. 'There's never been a necklace like this before, not in all the world. I'm sure there hasn't.' And then, 'You can leave me there, Mum, and I'll walk back. It's only a mile or so along the cliff path and half a mile back across the fields. I've done it before on my own. It's not far.'

There was a thundering on the stairs and a sudden rude invasion of the kitchen. Cherry was surrounded by her four brothers who leant over the table in mock appreciation of her necklace.

'Ooh, pretty.'

'Do they come in other colours? I mean, pink's not my colour.'

'Who's it for? An elephant?'

'It's for a giant,' said Cherry. 'It's a giant's necklace, and it's still not big enough.'

It was the perfect answer, an answer she knew would send her brothers into fits of laughter. She loved to make them laugh at her and could do it at the drop of a hat. Of course she no more believed in giants than they did, but if it tickled them pink to believe she did, then why not pretend?

She turned on them, fists flailing and chased them back up the stairs, her eyes burning with simulated fury. 'Just 'cos you don't believe in anything 'cept motorbikes and football and all that rubbish, just 'cos you're great big, fat, ignorant pigs . . .' She hurled insults up the stairs, and the worse the insult the more they loved it.

Boat Cove just below Zennor Head was the beach they had found and occupied. Every year for as long as Cherry could remember they had rented the same granite cottage, set back in the fields below the Eagle's Nest and every year they came to the same beach because no one else did. In two weeks not another soul had ventured down the winding track through the bracken from the coastal path. It was a long climb down and a very much longer one up. The beach itself was almost hidden from the path that ran along the cliff top a hundred feet above. It was private and perfect and theirs. The boys swam in amongst the rocks, diving and snorkelling for hours on end. Her mother and father would sit side by side on stripey deck chairs. She would read endlessly and he would close his eyes against the sun and dream for hours on end.

Cherry moved away from them and clambered over the rocks to a narrow strip of sand in the cove beyond the rocks, and here it was that she mined for the cowrie shells. In the gritty sand under the cliff face she had found a particularly rich deposit. She was looking for pink cowrie shells of a uniform length, colour and shape – that was what took the time. Occasionally the boys would swim around the rocks and in to her little beach, emerging from the sea all goggled and flippered to mock her. But as she paid them little attention they soon tired and went away again. She knew time was running short. This was her very last chance to find enough shells to complete the giant's necklace, and it had to be done.

The sea was calmer that day than she had ever seen it. The heat beat down from a windless, cloudless sky; even the gulls and kittiwakes seemed to be silenced by the sun. Cherry searched on, stopping only for a picnic lunch of pasties and tomatoes with the family before returning at once to her shells.

In the end the heat proved too much for her mother and father, who left the beach earlier than usual in mid-afternoon to begin to tidy up the cottage. The boys soon followed because they had tired of finding miniature crabs and seaweed instead of the sunken wrecks and treasure they had been seeking. So, by tea-time Cherry was left on her own on the beach with strict instructions to keep her hat on, not to bathe alone and to be back well before dark. She had calculated she needed one hundred and fifty more cowrie shells and so far she had only found eighty. She would be back, she insisted, when she had finished collecting enough shells and not before.

Had she not been so immersed in her search, sifting the shells through her fingers, she would have noticed the dark grey bank of cloud rolling in from the Atlantic. She would have noticed the white horses gathering out at sea and the tide moving remorselessly in to cover the rocks between her and Boat Cove. When the clouds cut off the warmth from the sun as evening came on and the sea turned grey, she shivered with cold and put on her sweater and jeans. She did look up then and saw the angry sea, but she saw no threat in that and did not look back over her shoulder to Boat Cove. She was aware that time was running out so she went down on her knees again and dug feverishly in the sand. She had to collect thirty more shells.

It was the baleful sound of the foghorn somewhere out at sea beyond Gunnards Head that at last forced Cherry to take some account of the incoming tide. She looked for the rocks she would have to clamber over to reach Boat Cove again and the winding track that would take her up to the cliff path and safety, but they were gone. Where they should have been, the sea was already driving in against the cliff face. She was cut off. In a confusion of wonder and fear she looked out to sea at the heaving ocean that moved in towards her, seeing it now as a writhing grey monster breathing its fury on the rocks with every pounding wave.

Still Cherry did not forget her shells, but wrapping them inside her towel she tucked them into her sweater and waded out through the surf towards the rocks. If she timed it right, she reasoned, she could scramble back over them and into the Cove as the surf retreated. She reached the first of the rocks without too much difficulty; the sea here seemed to be protected from the force of the ocean by the rocks further out. Holding fast to the first rock she came to and with the sea up around her waist, she waited for the next incoming wave to break and retreat. The wave was unexpectedly impotent and fell limply on the rocks around her. She knew her moment had come and took it. She was not to know that piling up far out at sea was the first of the giant storm waves that had gathered several hundred miles out in the Atlantic, bringing with it all the momentum and violence of the deep ocean.

The rocks were slippery underfoot and more than once Cherry slipped down into seething white rock pools where she had played so often when the tide was out. But she struggled on until, finally, she had climbed high enough to be able to see the thin strip of sand that was all that was left of Boat Cove. It was only a few yards away, so close. Until now she had been crying involuntarily; but now, as she recognised the little path up through the bracken, her heart was lifted with hope and anticipation. She knew that the worst was over, that if the sea would only hold back she would reach the sanctuary of the Cove.

She turned and looked behind her to see how far away the next wave was, just to reassure herself that she had enough time. But the great surge of green water was on her before she could register either disappointment or fear. She was hurled back against the rock below her and covered at once by the sea.

She was conscious as she went down that she was drowning, but she still clutched her shells against her chest and hoped she had enough of them at last to finish the giant's necklace. Those were her last thoughts before the sea took her away.

Cherry lay on her side where the tide had lifted her and coughed until her lungs were clear. She woke as the sea came in once again and frothed around her legs. She rolled on her back, feeling the salt spray on her face and saw that it was night. The sky above her was dashed with stars and the moon rode through the clouds.

She scrambled to her feet, one hand still holding her precious shells close to her. Instinctively she backed away from the sea and looked around her. With growing dismay she saw that she had been thrown back on the wrong side of the rocks, that she was not in Boat Cove. The tide had left only a few feet of sand and rock between her and the cliff face. There was no way back through the sea to safety.

She turned round to face the cliff that she realised now would be her last hope, for she remembered that this little beach vanished completely at high tide. If she stayed where she was she would surely be swept away again and this time she might not be so fortunate. But the cold seemed to have calmed her and she reasoned more deliberately now, wondering why she had not tried climbing the cliff before. She had hurried into her first attempt at escape and it had very nearly cost her her life. She would wait this time until the sea forced her up the cliff. Perhaps the tide would not come in that far. Perhaps they would be looking for her by now. It was dark. Surely they would be searching. Surely they must find her soon. After all, they knew where she was. Yes, she thought, best just to wait and hope.

She settled down on a ledge of rock that was the first step up on to the cliff face, drew her knees up to her chin to keep out the chill, and waited. She watched as the sea crept ever closer, each wave lashing her with spray and eating away gradually at the beach. She closed her eyes and prayed, hoping against hope that when she opened them the sea would be retreating. But her prayers went unanswered and the sea came in to cover the beach. Once or twice she thought she heard voices above her on the cliff path, but when she called out no one came. She continued to shout for help every few minutes, forgetting it was futile against the continuous roar and hiss of the waves. A pair of raucous white gulls flew down from the cliffs to investigate her and she called to them for help, but they did not seem to understand and wheeled away into the night.

Cherry stayed sitting on her rock until the waves threatened to dislodge her and then reluctantly she began her climb. She would go as far as she needed to and no further. She had scanned the first few feet above for footholds and it did look quite a simple climb to begin with, and so it proved. But her hands were numbed with cold and her legs began to tremble with the strain almost at once. She could see that the ledge she had now reached was the last deep one visible on the cliff face. The shells in her sweater were restricting her freedom of movement so she decided she would leave them there. Wrapped tight in the towel they would be quite safe. She took the soaking bundle out of her sweater and placed it carefully against the rock face on the ledge beside her, pushing it in as far as it would go. 'I'll be back for you,' she said, and reached up for the next lip of rock. Just below her the sea crashed against the cliff as if it wanted to suck her from the rock face and claim her once again. Cherry determined not to look down but to concentrate on the climb.

At first, she imagined that the glow above her was from a torch. She shouted and screamed until she was weak from the effort of it. But although no answering call came from the night, the light remained pale and beckoning, wider than that of a torch. With renewed hope Cherry found enough strength to inch her way up the cliff, until she reached the entrance to a narrow cave. It was filled with a flickering yellow light like that of a candle shaken by the wind. She hauled herself up into the mouth of the cave and sat down exhausted, looking back down at the furious sea frothing beneath her. She laughed aloud in triumph. She was safe! She had defied the sea and won! Her one regret was that she had had to leave her cowrie shells behind. She would fetch them tomorrow after the tide had gone down again.

For the first time now she began to think of her family and how worried they would be, but the thought of walking in through the front door all dripping and dramatic made her almost choke with excitement.

As she reached forward to brush a sharp stone from the sole of her foot, Cherry noticed that the narrow entrance to the cave was half sealed in. She ran her fingers over the stones and cement to make sure, for the light was poor. It was at that moment that she recognised exactly where she was. She recalled now the giant fledgling cuckoo one of her brothers had spotted being fed by a tiny rock pipit earlier in the holidays, how they had quarrelled over the binoculars and how, when she had finally usurped them and made her escape across the rocks, she had found the cuckoo perched at the entrance to a narrow cave some way up the cliff face from the beach.

She had asked about the man-made walling, and her father had told her of the old tin mines whose lodes and adits criss-crossed the entire coastal area around Zennor. This one, he said, might have been the mine they called Wheel North Grylls, and he thought the adit must have been walled up to prevent the seas from entering the mine in a storm. It was said there had been an accident in the mine only a few years after it was opened over a hundred years before, and that the mine had had to close soon after when the mine owners ran out of money to make the necessary repairs. The entire story came back to her now, and she wondered where the cuckoo was and whether the rock pipit had died with the effort of keeping the fledgling alive. Tin mines, she thought, lead to the surface, and the way home. That thought and her natural inquisitiveness about the source of light persuaded her to her feet and into the tunnel.

The adit became narrower and lower as she crept forward, so that she had to go down on her hands and knees, sometimes flat on her stomach. Although she was out of the wind now, it seemed colder. She felt she was moving downwards for a minute or two, for the blood was coming to her head and her weight was heavy on her hands. Then, quite suddenly, she found the ground levelling out and saw a large tunnel ahead of her. There was no doubt as to which way she should turn, for one way the tunnel was black, and the other way was lighted with candles that lined the lode wall as far as she could see. She called out, 'Anyone there? Anyone there?' She paused to listen for the reply; but all she could hear now was the muffled roar of the sea and the continuous echoing of dripping water.

The tunnel widened now and she found she could walk upright again; but her feet hurt against the stone and so she moved slowly, feeling her way gently with each foot. She had gone only a short distance when she heard the tapping for the first time, distinct and rhythmic, a sound that was instantly recognisable as hammering. It became sharper and noticeably more metallic as she moved up the tunnel. She could hear the distant murmur of voices and the sound of falling stone. Even before she came out of the tunnel and into the vast cave she knew she had happened upon a working mine.

The cave was dark in all but one corner and here she could see two men bending to their work, their backs towards her. One of them was inspecting the rock face closely whilst the other swung his hammer with controlled power, pausing only to spit on his hands from time to time. They wore round hats with turned up brims that served also as candlesticks, for a lighted candle was fixed to each, the light dancing with the shadows along the cave walls as they worked.

Cherry watched for some moments until she made up her mind what to do. She longed to rush up to them and tell of her escape and to ask them to take her to the surface, but a certain shyness overcame her and she held back. Her chance to interrupt came when they sat down against the rock face and opened their canteens. She was in the shadows and they still could not see her.

'Tea looks cold again,' one of them said gruffly. ''Tis always cold. I'm sure she makes it wi' cold water.'

'Oh stop your moaning, Father,' said the other, a younger voice, Cherry felt. 'She does her best. She's five little ones to look after and precious little to do it on. She does her best. You mustn't keep on at her so. It upsets her. She does her best.'

'So she does, lad, so she does. And so for that matter do I, but that don't stop her moaning at me and it'll not stop me moaning at her. If we didn't moan at each other, lad, we'd have precious little else to talk about, and that's a fact. She expects of it me, lad, and I expects it of her.'

'Excuse me,' Cherry said tentatively. She felt she had eavesdropped for long enough. She approached them slowly. 'Excuse me, but I've got a bit lost. I climbed the cliff, you see, 'cos I was cut off from the Cove. I was trying to get back, but I couldn't and I saw this light and so I climbed up. I want to get home and I wondered if you could help me get to the top?'

'Top?' said the older one, peering into the dark. 'Come closer, lad, where we can see you.'

'She's not a lad, Father. Are you blind? Can you not see 'tis a filly. 'Tis a young filly, all wet through from the sea. Come,' the young man said, standing up and beckoning Cherry in. 'Don't be afeared, little girl, we shan't harm you. Come on, you can have some of my tea if you like.'

They spoke their words in a manner Cherry had never heard before. It was not the usual Cornish burr, but heavier and rougher in tone, more old-fashioned somehow. There were so many questions in her mind.

'But I thought the mine was closed a hundred years ago,' she said nervously. 'That's what I was told, anyway.'

'Well, you was told wrong,' said the old man, whom Cherry could see more clearly now under his candle. His eyes were white and set far back in his head, unnaturally so, she thought, and his lips and mouth seemed a vivid red in the candlelight.

'Closed, closed indeed, does it look closed to you? D'you think we're digging for worms? Over four thousand tons of tin last year and nine thousand of copper ore, and you ask is the mine closed? Over twenty fathoms below the sea this mine goes. We'll dig right out under the ocean, halfway to 'Merica afore we close down this mine.'

He spoke passionately now, almost angrily, so that Cherry felt she had offended him.

'Hush, Father,' said the young man taking off his jacket and wrapping it round Cherry's shoulders. 'She doesn't want to hear all about that. She's cold and wet.

Can't you see? Now let's make a little fire to warm her through. She's shivered right through to her bones. You can see she is.'

'They all are,' said the old tinner pulling himself to his feet. 'They all are.' And he shuffled past her into the dark. 'I'll fetch the wood,' he muttered, and then added, 'for all the good it'll do.'

'What does he mean?' Cherry asked the young man, for whom she felt an instant liking. 'What did he mean by that?'

'Oh pay him no heed, little girl,' he said. 'He's an old man now and tired of the mine. We're both tired of it, but we're proud of it see, and we've nowhere else to go, nothing else to do.'

He had a kind voice that was reassuring to Cherry. He seemed somehow to know the questions she wanted to ask, for he answered them now without her ever asking.

'Sit down by me while you listen, girl,' he said.

'Father will make a fire to warm you and I shall tell you how we come to be here. You won't be afeared now, will you?'

Cherry looked up into his face which was younger than she had expected from his voice; but like his father's, the eyes seemed sad and deep set, yet they smiled at her gently and she smiled back.

'That's my girl. It was a new mine this, promising everyone said. The best tin in Cornwall and that means the best tin in the world. 1865 it started up and they were looking for tinners, and so Father found a cottage down by Treveal and came to work here. I was already fourteen, so I joined him down the mine. We prospered and the mine prospered, to start with. Mother and the little children had full bellies and there was talk of sinking a fresh shaft. Times were good and promised to be better.'

Cherry sat transfixed as the story of the disaster unfolded. She heard how they had been trapped by a fall of rock, about how they had worked to pull them away, but behind every rock was another rock and another rock. She heard how they had never even heard any sound of rescue. They had died, he said, in two days or so because the air was bad and because there was too little of it.

'Father has never accepted it; he still thinks he's alive, that he goes home to Mother and the little children each evening. But he's dead, just like me. I can't tell him though, for he'd not understand and it would break his heart if he ever knew.'

'So you aren't real. I'm just imagining all this. You're just a dream.'

'No dream, my girl,' said the young man laughing

out loud. 'No more'n we're imagining you. We're real right enough, but we're dead and have been for a hundred years and more. Ghosts, spirits, that's what living folk call us. Come to think of it, that's what I called us when I was alive.'

Cherry was on her feet suddenly and backing away.

'No need to be afeared, little girl,' said the young man holding out his hand towards her. 'We won't harm you. No one can harm you, not now. Look, he's started the fire already. Come over and warm yourself. Come, it'll be all right, girl. We'll look after you. We'll help you.'

'But I want to go home,' Cherry said, feeling the panic rising to her voice and trying to control it. 'I know you're kind, but I want to go home. My mother will be worried about me. They'll be out looking for me. Your light saved my life and I want to thank you. But I must go else they'll worry themselves sick, I know they will.'

'You going back home?' the young man asked, and then he nodded. 'I s'pose you'll want to see your family again.'

"Course I am,' said Cherry perplexed by the question. ''Course I do.'

"Tis a pity,' he said sadly. 'Everyone passes through and no one stays. They all want to go home, but then so do I. You'll want me to guide you to the surface I s'pose.'

'I'm not the first then?' Cherry said. 'There's been others climb up into the mine to escape from the sea? You've saved lots of people.'

'A few,' said the tinner nodding. 'A few.'

'You're a kind person,' Cherry said, warming to the sadness in the young man's voice. 'I never thought ghosts would be kind.'

'We're just people, people who've passed on,' replied the young man, taking her elbow and leading her towards the fire. 'There's nice people and there's nasty people. It's the same if you're alive or if you're dead. You're a nice person, I can tell that, even though I haven't known you for long. I'm sad because I should like to be alive again with my friends and go rabbiting or blackberrying up by the chapel near Treveal like I used to. The sun always seemed to be shining then. After it happened I used to go up to the surface and move amongst the people in the village. I went often to see my family, but if I spoke to them they never seemed to hear me, and of course they can't see you. You can see them, but they can't see you. That's the worst of it. So I don't go up much now, just to collect wood for the fire and a bit of food now and then. I stay down here with Father in the mine and we work away day after day. From time to time someone like you comes up the tunnel from the sea and lightens our darkness. I shall be sad when you go.'

The old man was hunched over the fire rubbing his hands and holding them out over the heat.

'Not often we have a fire,' he said, his voice more spritely now. 'Only on special occasions. Birthdays, of course, we always have a fire on birthdays back at the cottage. Martha's next. You don't know her; she's my only daughter – she'll be eight on September 10th. She's been poorly, you know – her lungs, that's what the doctor said.' He sighed deeply. ''Tis dreadful damp in the cottage. 'Tis well nigh impossible to keep it out.' There was a tremor in the old man's voice that betrayed his emotion. He looked up at Cherry and she could see the tears in his eyes. 'She looks a bit like you, my dear, raven-haired and as pretty as a picture; but not so tall, not so tall. Come closer, my dear, you'll be warmer that way.'

Cherry sat with them by the fire till it died away to nothing. She longed to go, to get home amongst the living, but the old man talked on of his family and their little one-roomed cottage with a ladder to the bedroom where they all huddled together for warmth, of his friends that used to meet in the Tinners' Arms every evening. There were tales of wrecking and smuggling, and all the while the young man sat silent, until there was a lull in the story.

'Father,' he said. 'I think our little friend would like to go home now. Shall I take her up as I usually do?' The old man nodded and waved his hand in dismissal.

'Come back and see us sometime, if you've a mind to,' he said, and then put his face in his hands.

'Goodbye,' said Cherry. 'Thank you for the fire and for helping me. I won't forget you.' But the old man never replied.

The journey through the mine was long and difficult. She held fast to the young tinner's waist as they walked silently through the dark tunnels, stopping every now and then to climb a ladder to the lode above until finally they could look up the shaft above them and see the daylight.

'It's dawn,' said the young man, looking up.

'I'll be back in time for breakfast,' said Cherry setting her foot on the ladder.

'You'll remember me?' the young tinner asked, and Cherry nodded, unable to speak through her tears. She felt a strange affinity with him and his father. 'And if you should ever need me, come back again. You may need me and I shall be here. I go nowhere else.'

'Thank you,' said Cherry. 'I won't forget. I doubt anyone is going to believe me when I tell them about you. No one believes in ghosts, not up there.'

'I doubt it too. Be happy, little friend,' he said. And

he was gone, back into the tunnel. Cherry waited until the light from the candle in his hat had vanished and then turned eagerly to the ladder and began to climb up towards the light.

She found herself in a place she knew well, high on the moor by Zennor Quoit. She stood by the ruined mine workings and looked down at the sleeping village shrouded in mist, and the calm blue sea beyond. The storm had passed and there was scarcely a breath of wind even on the moor. It was only ten minutes' walk down through the bracken, across the road by the Eagle's Nest and down the farm track to the cottage where her family would be waiting. She began to run, but the clothes were still heavy and wet and she was soon reduced to a fast walk. All the while she was determining where she would begin her story, wondering how much they would believe. At the top of the lane she stopped to consider how best to make her entrance. Should she ring the bell and be found standing there, or should she just walk in and surprise them there at breakfast? She longed to see the joy on their faces, to feel the warmth of their arms round her and to bask once again in their affection.

She saw as she came round the corner by the cottage that there was a long blue Land Rover parked in the lane, bristling with aerials. *'Coastguard'* she read on the side. As she came down the steps she noticed that the back door of the cottage was open and she could hear voices inside. She stole in on tiptoe. The kitchen was full of uniformed men drinking tea, and around the table sat her family, dejection and despair etched on every face. They hadn't seen her yet. One of the uniformed men had put down his cup and was speaking. His voice was low and hushed.

'You're sure the towel is hers, no doubts about it?'

Cherry's mother shook her head.

'It's her towel,' she said quietly, 'and they are her shells. She must have put them up there, must have been the last thing she did.'

Cherry saw her shells spread out on the open towel and stifled a shout of joy.

'We have to say,' he went on. 'We have to say then, most regrettably, that the chances of finding your daughter alive now are very slim. It seems she must have tried to climb the cliff to escape the heavy seas and fallen in. We've scoured the cliff top for miles in both directions and covered the entire beach, and there's no sign of her. She must have been washed out to sea. We must conclude that she is missing. We have to presume that she is drowned.'

Cherry could listen no longer but burst into the room shouting.

'I'm home, I'm home. Look at me, I'm not drowned at all. I'm here! I'm home!'

The tears were running down her face.

But no one in the room even turned to look in her direction. Her brothers cried openly, one of them clutching the giant's necklace.

'But it's me,' she shouted again. 'Me, can't you see? It's me and I've come back. I'm all right. Look at me.'

But no one did, and no one heard.

The giant's necklace lay spread out on the table.

'So she'll never finish it after all,' said her mother softly. 'Poor Cherry. Poor dear Cherry.'

And in that one moment Cherry knew and understood that she was right, that she would never finish her necklace, that she belonged no longer with the living but had passed on beyond.

My Father is a Polar Bear

This story is a tissue of truth – mostly. As with many of my stories, I have woven truths together and made from them a truth stranger than fiction. My father was a polar bear – honestly.

Tracking down a polar bear shouldn't be that difficult. You just follow the pawprints – easy enough for any competent Innuit. My father is a polar bear. Now if you had a father who was a polar bear, you'd be curious, wouldn't you? You'd go looking for him. That's what I did, I went looking for him, and I'm telling you he wasn't at all easy to find.

In a way I was lucky, because I always had two fathers. I had a father who *was* there – I called him Douglas – and one who wasn't there, the one I'd never even met – the polar bear one. Yet in a way he was there. All the time I was growing up he was there inside my head. But he wasn't only in my head, he was at the bottom of our Start-Rite shoebox, our secret treasure box, with the rubber bands round it, which I kept hidden at the bottom of the cupboard in our bedroom. So how, you might ask, does a polar bear fit into a shoebox? I'll tell you.

My big brother Terry first showed me the magazine under the bedclothes, by torchlight, in 1948 when I was five years old. The magazine was called *Theatre World*. I couldn't read it at the time, but he could. (He was two years older than me, and already mad about acting and the theatre and all that – he still is.) He had saved up all his pocket money to buy it. I thought he was crazy. 'A shilling! You can get about a hundred lemon sherbets for that down at the shop,' I told him.

Terry just ignored me and turned to page twenty-seven. He read it out: 'The Snow Queen, a dramat – something or other – of Hans Andersen's famous story, by the Young Vic Company.' And there was a large black and white photograph right across the page – a photograph of two fierce looking polar bears baring their teeth and about to eat two children, a boy and a girl, who looked very frightened.

'Look at the polar bears,' said Terry. 'You see that one on the left, the fatter one? That's our dad, our real dad. It says his name and everything – Peter Van

Diemen. But you're not to tell. Not Douglas, not even Mum, promise?'

'My dad's a polar bear?' I said. As you can imagine I was a little confused.

'Promise you won't tell,' he went on, 'or I'll give you a Chinese burn.'

Of course I wasn't going to tell, Chinese burn or no Chinese burn. I was hardly going to go to school the next day and tell everyone that I had a polar bear for a father, was I? And I certainly couldn't tell my mother, because I knew she never liked it if I ever asked about my real father. She always insisted that Douglas was the only father I had. I knew he wasn't, not really. So did she, so did Terry, so did Douglas. But for some reason that was always a complete mystery to me, everyone in the house pretended that he was.

Some background might be useful here. I was born, I later found out, when my father was a soldier in Baghdad during the Second World War. (You didn't know there were polar bears in Baghdad, did you?) Sometime after that my mother met and fell in love with a dashing young officer in the Royal Marines called Douglas Macleish. All this time, evacuated to the Lake District away from the bombs, blissfully unaware of the war and Douglas, I was learning to walk and talk and do my business in the right place at the right time.

So my father came home from the war to discover that his place in my mother's heart had been taken. He did all he could to win her back. He took her away on a week's cycling holiday in Suffolk to see if he could rekindle the light of their love. But it was hopeless. By the end of the week they had come to an amicable arrangement. My father would simply disappear, because he didn't want to 'get in the way'. They would get divorced quickly and quietly, so that Terry and I could be brought up as a new family with Douglas as our father. Douglas would adopt us and give us Macleish as our surname. All my father insisted upon was that Terry and I should keep Van Diemen as our middle name. That's what happened. They divorced. My father disappeared, and at the age of three I became Andrew Van Diemen Macleish. It was a mouthful then and it's a mouthful now.

So Terry and I had no actual memories of our father whatsoever. I do have vague recollections of standing on a railway bridge somewhere near Earl's Court in London, where we lived, with Douglas' sister – Aunt Betty, as I came to know her – telling us that we had a brand new father who'd be looking after us from now on. I was really not that concerned, not at the time. I was much more interested in the train that was chuffing along under the bridge, wreathing us in a fog of smoke.

My first father, my real father, my missing father, became a taboo person, a big hush hush taboo person that no one ever mentioned, except for Terry and me. For us he soon became a sort of secret phantom father. We used to whisper about him under the blankets at night. Terry would sometimes go snooping in my mother's desk and he'd find things out about him. 'He's an actor,' Terry told me one night. 'Our dad's an actor, just like Mum is, just like I'm going to be.'

It was only a couple of weeks later that he brought the theatre magazine home. After that we'd take it out again and look at our polar bear father. It took some time, I remember, before the truth of it dawned on me – I don't think Terry can have explained it very well. If he had, I'd have understood it much sooner – I'm sure I would. The truth, of course – as I think you might have guessed by now – was that my father was both an actor *and* a polar bear at one and the same time.

Douglas went out to work a lot and when he was home he was a bit silent, so we didn't really get to know him. But we did get to know Aunty Betty. Aunty Betty simply adored us, and she loved giving us treats. She wanted to take us on a special Christmas treat, she said. Would we like to go to the zoo? Would we like to go to the pantomime? There was *Dick Whittington* or *Puss in Boots*. We could choose whatever we liked.

Quick as a flash, Terry said, 'The Snow Queen. We want to go to *The Snow Queen*.'

So there we were a few days later, Christmas Eve 1948, sitting in the stalls at a matinee performance of *The Snow Queen* at the Young Vic theatre, waiting, waiting for the moment when the polar bears come on. We didn't have to wait for long. Terry nudged me and pointed, but I knew already which polar bear my father had to be. He was the best one, the snarliest one, the growliest one, the scariest one. Whenever he came on he really looked as if he was going to eat someone, anyone. He looked mean and hungry and savage, just the way a polar bear should look.

I have no idea whatsoever what happened in *The Snow Queen*. I just could not take my eyes off my polar bear father's curling claws, his slavering tongue, his killer eyes. My father was without doubt the finest polar bear actor the world had ever seen. When the great red curtains closed at the end and opened again for the actors to take their bows, I clapped so hard that my hands hurt. Three more curtain calls and the curtains stayed closed. The safety curtain came down and my father was cut off from me, gone, gone for ever. I'd never see him again.

Terry had other ideas. Everyone was getting up, but Terry stayed sitting. He was staring at the safety curtain as if in some kind of trance. 'I want to meet the polar bears,' he said quietly.

Aunty Betty laughed. 'They're not bears, dear, they're actors, just actors, people acting. And you can't meet them, it's not allowed.'

'I want to meet the polar bears,' Terry repeated. So did I, of course, so I joined in. 'Please, Aunty Betty,' I pleaded. 'Please.'

'Don't be silly. You two, you do get some silly notions sometimes. Have a Choc Ice instead. Get your coats on now.' So we each got a Choc Ice. But that wasn't the end of it.

We were in the foyer caught in the crush of the crowd when Aunty Betty suddenly noticed that Terry was missing. She went loopy. Aunty Betty always wore a fox stole, heads still attached, round her shoulders. Those poor old foxes looked every bit as pop-eyed and frantic as she did, as she plunged through the crowd, dragging me along behind her and calling for Terry.

Gradually the theatre emptied. Still no Terry. There was quite a to-do, I can tell you. Policemen were called in off the street. All the programme sellers joined in the search, everyone did. Of course, I'd worked it out. I knew exactly where Terry had gone, and what he was up to. By now Aunty Betty was sitting down in the foyer and sobbing her heart out. Then, cool as a cucumber, Terry appeared from nowhere, just wandered into the foyer. Aunty Betty crushed him to her, in a great hug. Then she went loopy all over again, telling him what a naughty, naughty boy he was, going off like that. 'Where were you? Where have you been?' she cried.

'Yes, young man,' said one of the policemen. 'That's something we'd all like to know as well.'

I remember to this day exactly what Terry said, the very words: 'Jimmy riddle. I just went for a jimmy riddle.' For just a moment he even had me believing him. What an actor! Brilliant.

We were on the bus home, right at the front on the top deck where you can guide the bus round corners all by yourself – all you have to do is steer hard on the white bar in front of you. Aunty Betty was sitting a couple of rows behind us. Terry made quite sure she wasn't looking. Then, very surreptitiously, he took something out from under his coat and showed me. The programme. Signed right across it were these words, which Terry read out to me:

> *'To Terry and Andrew,*
> *With love from your polar bear father, Peter. Keep*
> *happy.'*

Night after night I asked Terry about him, and night after night under the blankets he'd tell me the story again, about how he'd gone into the dressing-room and found our father sitting there in his polar bear costume with his head off (if you know what I mean), all hot and sweaty. Terry said he had a very round, very smiley face, and that he laughed just like a bear would laugh, a sort of deep bellow of a laugh – when he'd got over the surprise that is. Terry described him as looking like 'a giant pixie in a bearskin'.

For ever afterwards I always held it against Terry that he never took me with him that day down to the dressing-room to meet my polar bear father. I was so envious. Terry had a memory of him now, a real memory. And I didn't. All I had were a few words and a signature on a theatre programme from someone I'd never even met, someone who to me was part polar bear, part actor, part pixie – not at all easy to picture in my head as I grew up.

Picture another Christmas Eve fourteen years later. Upstairs, still at the bottom of my cupboard, my polar bear father in the magazine in the Start-Rite shoebox; and with him all our accumulated childhood treasures: the signed programme, a battered champion conker (a sixty-fiver!), six silver ball-bearings, four greenish silver threepenny bits (Christmas pudding treasure trove), a

Red Devil throat pastille tin with three of my milk teeth cushioned in yellowy cotton wool, and my collection of twenty-seven cowrie shells gleaned over many summers from the beach on Samson in the Scilly Isles. Downstairs, the whole family were gathered in the sitting-room: my mother, Douglas, Terry and my two sisters (half-sisters really, but of course no one ever called them that), Aunty Betty, now married, with twin daughters, my cousins, who were truly awful – I promise you. We were decorating the tree, or rather the twins were fighting over every single dingly-dangly glitter ball, every strand of tinsel. I was trying to fix up the Christmas tree lights which, of course, wouldn't work – again – whilst Aunty Betty was doing her best to avert a war by bribing the dreadful cousins away from the tree with a Mars bar each. It took a while, but in the end she got both of them up on to her lap, and soon they were stuffing themselves contentedly with Mars bars. Blessed peace.

This was the very first Christmas we had had the television. Given half a chance we'd have had it on all the time. But, wisely enough I suppose, Douglas had rationed us to just one programme a day over Christmas. He didn't want the Christmas celebrations interfered with by 'that thing in the corner', as he called it. By common consent, we had chosen the Christmas Eve film on the BBC at five o'clock.

Five o'clock was a very long time coming that day, and when at last Douglas got up and turned on the television, it seemed to take for ever to warm up. Then, there it was on the screen: *Great Expectations* by Charles Dickens. The half-mended lights were at once discarded, the decorating abandoned, as we all settled down to watch in rapt anticipation. Maybe you know the moment: Young Pip is making his way through the graveyard at dusk, mist swirling around him, an owl screeching, gravestones rearing out of the gloom, branches like ghoulish fingers whipping at him as he passes, reaching out to snatch him. He moves through the graveyard timorously, tentatively, like a frightened fawn. Every snap of a twig, every barking fox, every aarking heron sends shivers into our very souls.

Suddenly, a face! A hideous face, a monstrous face, looms up from behind a gravestone. Magwitch, the escaped convict, ancient, craggy and crooked, with long white hair and a straggly beard. A wild man with wild eyes, the eyes of a wolf.

The cousins screamed in unison, long and loud, which broke the tension for all of us and made us laugh. All except my mother.

'Oh my God,' she breathed, grasping my arm. 'That's your father! It is. It's him. It's Peter.'

All the years of pretence, the whole long conspiracy

of silence were undone in that one moment. The drama on the television paled into sudden insignificance. The hush in the room was palpable.

Douglas coughed. 'I think I'll fetch some more logs,' he said. And my two half sisters went out with him, in solidarity I think. So did Aunty Betty and the twins; and that left my mother, Terry and me alone together.

I could not take my eyes off the screen. After a while I said to Terry, 'He doesn't look much like a pixie to me.'

'Doesn't look much like a polar bear either,' Terry replied. At Magwitch's every appearance I tried to see through his make-up (I just hoped it *was* make-up!) to discover how my father really looked. It was impossible. My polar bear father, my pixie father had become my convict father.

Until the credits came up at the end my mother never said a word. Then all she said was, 'Well, the potatoes won't peel themselves, and I've got the brussel sprouts to do as well.' Christmas was a very subdued affair that year, I can tell you.

They say you can't put a genie back in the bottle. Not true. No one in the family ever spoke of the incident afterwards – except Terry and me of course. Everyone behaved as if it had never happened. Enough was enough. Terry and I decided it was time to broach the whole forbidden subject with our mother, in private. We waited until the furore of Christmas was over, and caught her alone in the kitchen one evening. We asked her point blank to tell us about him, our 'first' father, our 'missing' father.

'I don't want to talk about him,' she said. She wouldn't even look at us. 'All I know is that he lives somewhere in Canada now. It was another life. I was another person then. It's not important.' We tried to press her, but that was all she would tell us.

Soon after this I became very busy with my own life, and for some years I thought very little about my convict father, my polar bear father. By the time I was thirty I was married with two sons, and was a teacher trying to become a writer, something I had never dreamt I could be.

Terry had become an actor, something he had always been quite sure he would be. He rang me very late one night in a high state of excitement. 'You'll never guess,' he said. 'He's here! Peter! Our dad. He's here, in England. He's playing in *Henry IV, Part II* in Chichester. I've just read a rave review. He's Falstaff. Why don't we go down there and give him the surprise of his life?'

So we did. The next weekend we went down to Chichester together. I took my family with me. I wanted them to be there for this. He was a wonderful

41

Falstaff, big and boomy, rumbustuous and raunchy, yet full of pathos. My two boys (ten and eight) kept whispering at me every time he came on. 'Is that him? Is that him?' Afterwards we went round to see him in his dressing-room. Terry said I should go in first, and on my own. 'I had my turn a long time ago, if you remember,' he said. 'Best if he sees just one of us to start with, I reckon.'

My heart was in my mouth. I had to take a very deep breath before I knocked on that door. 'Enter.' He sounded still jovial, still Falstaffian. I went in.

He was sitting at his dressing-table in his vest and braces, boots and britches, and humming to himself as he rubbed off his make-up. We looked at each other in the mirror. He stopped humming, and swivelled round to face me. For some moments I just stood there looking at him. Then I said, 'Were you a polar bear once, a long time ago in London?'

'Yes.'

'And were you once the convict in *Great Expectations* on the television?'

'Yes.'

'Then I think I'm your son,' I told him.

There was a lot of hugging in his dressing-room that night, not enough to make up for all those missing years, maybe. But it was a start.

My mother's dead now, bless her heart, but I still have two fathers. I get on well enough with Douglas, I always have done in a detached sort of way. He's done his best by me, I know that; but in all the years I've known him he's never once mentioned my other father. It doesn't matter now. It's history best left crusted over I think.

We see my polar bear father – I still think of him as that – every year or so, whenever he's over from Canada. He's well past eighty now, still acting for six months of every year – a real trouper. My children and my grandchildren always call him Grandpa Bear because of his great bushy beard (the same one he grew for Falstaff!), and because they all know the story of their grandfather, I suppose.

Recently I wrote a story about a polar bear. I can't imagine why. He's upstairs now reading it to my smallest granddaughter. I can hear him a-snarling and a-growling just as proper polar bears do. Takes him back, I should think. Takes me back, that's for sure.

What Does It Feel Like?

Rwanda, Bosnia, Kosovo, East Timor. Ethnic cleansing seems as rife today as it has been throughout history. Yet in our oh-so-comfy England, it can seem a world away – 'just on the telly'. I once visited, by chance, a village in France called Oradour, the scene of a dreadful massacre in the Second World War. The French have preserved the place as the German occupiers left it: burnt out and stark. As a memorial. I wrote this to remind me, and others, that it is not 'just on the telly'. It is happening, now, as you read this.

Seven o'clock, and it was just an ordinary kind of autumn morning, much like any other. The mist covered the valley floor and the cows grazed along the river meadows. Sofia was still half-asleep. The wild roses smelt of apples. Sofia pulled a fat rosehip from the hedgerow and idly split it open with her thumbnail. It was packed with seeds. A perfect spider's web laced with mist linked the hedge to the gatepost. It trembled threateningly as she opened the gate into the meadow. She loved spiders' webs, but hated spiders.

Sofia sent the dog out to fetch in the cows and stayed leaning on the gate, her chin resting on her knuckles. Chewing nonchalantly, they meandered past her, ignoring her, all except Myrtle who glanced at her with baleful eyes and licked deep into her nose. 'Bad-tempered old cow,' Sofia muttered. And she followed Myrtle back along the lane towards the milking parlour. She could hear Mother singing inside, 'Raining in My Heart'. Buddy Holly again, always Buddy Holly.

Sofia wandered home, picking the last of the seeds out of the rosehip. She was deep in her thoughts. Mother did all the milking these days. She had done since Father went off with the other men to the war. He had been gone nearly three months now, and still there had been no news. No news was good news. Mother said that often. Sofia believed her, but she knew that was only because she needed to believe her. It was hope rather than belief. There was a photo of Father on top of the piano at home. A team photo, after the village won the local football league last year. He was the one with the droopy moustache and balding head, crouching down in the front and holding his arms out in triumph.

There had been little warning of his going. He'd just come out with it at breakfast one morning. Nan had tried to talk him out of it, but he was adamant. Mother and Nan held hands together and tried not to cry. 'There's five of us going from the village,' Father had said. 'We've got to, don't you see? Else the war will come here, and we none of us want that, do we?'

The fighting was somewhere down south a long way away, Sofia knew that much. People had talked of little else now for a year or more. She'd seen pictures of it on the television. There was the little girl without any legs, lying on a hospital bed. She'd never forgotten that. She never wanted to be without her legs, never. And at school, Mr Kovacs drew maps on the board, banged the desk, flashed his eyes and said that we had to fight for what was ours if we wanted to keep it. All of us had to fight if need be, he said. But until the day Father left, none of it seemed at all real to Sofia. Even now, she had seen no tanks or planes. She had heard no guns. She had asked Nan about the war – Mother didn't like to talk about it – about why Father was fighting.

'Because they want our land. They always have,' she'd said. 'And because we hate them. We always have. We've hated them for hundreds of years.'

'And do they hate us?' Sofia had asked.

'I suppose they must,' Nan had said.

Sofia remembered the last day Father had been with them. She had come home from school and he'd been there all smiling and smelling of the wood he'd been sawing. That evening was the last time they'd been milking together. She smiled as she recalled how Myrtle had whipped her mucky tail across Father's face. 'Bad-tempered old cow,' he'd said, wiping his face with the back of his hand. Sofia had laughed at the brown smudge on his face, and Father had chased her out of the parlour. She thought then of his strong, calloused hands and loved them.

Nan was calling her from her thoughts. She hurried her through her breakfast, grumbling all the time that the telephone was not working, that the electricity was cut off too.

'I can't understand it,' she said. 'Maybe there's thunder about, but it doesn't feel like thunder.' She sent her on her way to school with a whiskery kiss.

It was ten to eight on Sofia's watch. Plenty of time. The farm was just on the edge of the village, not far. Sofia scuffled through the leaves, all the way down the road. By the time she reached the village square, there were no leaves left to scuffle. So she limped, one foot on the pavement, one in the road. She liked doing that.

Sometimes, when no one was looking, she'd do the dance from *Singin' in the Rain*. This morning though, she couldn't. There were too many people around, but very little traffic on the move, she noticed, just a few bicycles. She crossed the road into the square. The café chairs were already out, and as usual Mighty Martha was scrubbing the pavement on her hands and knees. She looked up and blew the hair out of her face. Mighty Martha was the only famous person ever to be born in the village. She had won an Olympic silver medal for throwing the discus over twenty years before. Discus and medal hung proudly side by side on the café wall under a photo of Mighty Martha standing on a podium, smiling and waving. She was always smiling. That was why everyone wasn't just proud of her, they loved her too. It helped that she also happened to make the best apple cake in the entire world. That was why her café was always full, even at this early hour. She was smiling at Sofia now.

'Better hurry,' she called out. 'Kovacs will have your guts for garters if you're late.'

Sofia turned into School Lane. She could hear the bell going now. She'd just make it. But then she stopped. It wasn't only the bell she was hearing. There was a distant rumble that sounded like thunder. So Nan had been right. There was thunder about. Sofia looked up at the mountains. It couldn't be thunder. There were no dark clouds. In fact there were no clouds at all, just jagged white peaks sharp against a clear blue sky.

That was the moment Sofia remembered last night's geography homework: 'Mountain ranges of the world'. She'd left it behind. She fought back the panic rising inside her and tried to think. Both the choices open to her were bad ones. She could run home to fetch it and be late for school, very late; or she could tell Mr Kovacs that she'd left it at home by mistake, but then he wouldn't believe her. Either way Mr Kovacs would 'have her guts for garters'. Sofia chose what seemed to be the least painful option. She would fetch her homework, and on the way there and back, concoct some credible excuse for being late. She ran back across the square with Mighty Martha shouting after her, 'Where are you off to?' Sofia waved but did not reply.

The quickest way home was through the graveyard, but Sofia rarely took it. This morning she had to. She usually avoided the graveyard because Grandad had been buried there only two years before in the family grave and Nan went up there twice a week with fresh flowers. To pass the grave and see the flowers only made Sofia sad about Grandad all over again. There was a photograph of him on the grave that looked at her as she passed. She hated looking at it. She still half expected him to talk to her, which was silly and she knew it. Nonetheless she always hared past him before he had a chance to speak.

As she ran, her foot turned on a loose stone. She heard her ankle crack. It gave under her, and she fell heavily, grazing her knees and hands. She sat up to nurse her ankle, which was throbbing now with such a pain that she thought she might faint. When she finally looked up, Grandad was gazing at her sternly from his photograph. She tried to hold back her tears. He'd always hated her to cry. She rocked back and forth groaning, watching the blood from her knee trickle down her leg.

Her books were scattered all over the path, her English book face-down in a puddle. She was reaching for it when she heard the thunder again, much closer this time. For just a moment she thought it might be guns, but then she dismissed that at once. The war was down south, miles away, everyone said so. Mr Kovacs' maps said so. By now she was hearing an incongruous rattling and squeaking, more like the noise of a dozen tractors trailing their ploughs on the road. She stood up on her one good foot and looked down into the village.

Two tanks rumbled into the square from different ends of the village, engines roaring and smoking. Behind them came six open lorries. When they reached the square they all stopped. Soldiers jumped out. The engines died. The smoke lifted through the trees and a silence fell over the village. Doors opened, heads appeared at windows.

Mighty Martha stood alone in the square, her scrubbing brush in her hand. The soldiers were gazing around like tourists as the last of them climbed down out of the lorries. Mighty Martha's dog barked at them from the door of the café, his hackles raised. All the soldiers wore headbands, red headbands, except one who was wearing a beret, and there was a gunbelt round his waist like a cowboy. The soldiers – Sofia thought there must be perhaps thirty in all gathered around him – then wandered off in small groups into the narrow streets as if they were going to explore. They had their rifles slung over their shoulders. Sofia wondered if Father wore a red band round his head like they did. The man in the black beret leaned back against a tank, crossed his legs and lit up a cigarette. Mighty Martha stood watching him for a few moments. Then she dropped her scrubbing brush into the bucket, slapped her hands dry and strode into the café.

Sofia gathered up her books and hobbled down the path back towards the square. Mighty Martha would see to her ankle for her, like she had done once before when she'd come off her bike. She'd been a nurse once.

She knew about these things; and besides, Sofia wanted to know what was going on. She wanted to get a closer look at the tanks. The homework and Mr Kovacs had been forgotten.

She had got as far as the toilets on the corner of the square when she saw Martha coming out of the café. She was holding a rifle. Suddenly she stopped, brought it to her shoulder and pointed it at the cowboy soldier.

'This is our village,' she cried, 'and you will never take it from us, never.' A shot rang out and the rifle fell from Martha's hands. Her head twisted unnaturally on her neck and nodded loose for a moment like a puppet's head. Then she just collapsed, fell face forward on the cobbles and was still. The cowboy soldier was walking towards her, his pistol in his hand. He turned Martha over with the toe of his boot.

Sofia darted into the toilets, ran to the Ladies, closed the door behind her and bolted it. She sat down, squeezed her eyes tight shut and tried not to believe what she had just witnessed. She heard herself moaning and stopped breathing so that the moaning too would stop. But it did not. She knew then that it came from outside.

She climbed up on the toilet seat. The frosted window was a centimetre or two open. They were coming into the square from every corner of the square. Mr Kovacs and all the schoolchildren came in twos down School Lane, the soldiers hustling them along. The children seemed more bewildered than frightened, except little Ilic, who clutched Mr Kovacs' hand and cried openly. None of them had seen Martha yet. The cowboy soldier was climbing up on to a tank. He stood legs apart, thumbs hooked into his belt and watched as everyone was marshalled into the square.

The doctor was there, pushing old Mrs Marxova in her wheelchair. Swathed in a shawl, her face ashen, she was pointing down at Martha. Some people were still in their dressing-gowns and slippers. Stefan and Peter from the garage had their hands high in the air, a soldier behind them, jabbing them in their backs with his rifle barrel. Up the road from the bridge Sofia could see all the old folk from the retirement home, a couple of soldiers herding them along like cattle. They would pass by right underneath the toilet window. It was they who were moaning and wailing. Sofia drew back so she wouldn't be seen. She waited until they had gone and then peered out again.

The square was filling. The schoolchildren were gathered around Mr Kovacs who was talking to them, trying to reassure them, but the children had seen Martha. Everyone had seen Martha. Mrs Marxova held her hands over her eyes and was shaking her head.

The doctor was leaning over Martha and feeling her neck, then he was listening to her chest. After a while he took his jacket off and covered her face.

Little Ilic saw his mother and ran screaming across the square. One by one now the children ignored all Mr Kovacs' attempts to keep them together and went off to search for their mothers. Once found, they clung to them passionately as if they would never let go.

That was when Sofia saw Mother and Nan, arms linked, being marched into the square. All Sofia's neighbours were with them too. They'd even found Mr Dodovic who lived alone in his hut and kept his bees high up the mountainside. Like all the men, he too had his hands in the air. Mother went straight over to Mr Kovacs and took him by the arm. Mr Kovacs shook his head at her. Sofia longed to cry out, to run to her. But something inside her held her back. Everyone in the village was corralled in the square by now and surrounded by the soldiers.

A machine-gun was being set up on the steps of the post office and another by the garage on the corner. Mother was talking to the doctor and looking about her frantically. Nan had sat down in a chair outside the café and was staring blankly at Martha.

The cowboy soldier on the tank held up his hands. The hush was almost instantaneous. Even the children stopped crying, except for Mrs Dungonic's new baby. Mrs Dungonic picked her up and shushed her over her shoulder. The whole square was silent now, expectant.

'You have seen now what happens if you resist,' the cowboy soldier began. 'No one will come to help you. All the telephone lines are cut. All the roads are blocked. You will do what we say. We do not want to harm any more of you, but if you make us, we will. Have no doubt about it. We are simply moving you. This land does not belong to you. You have been squatting here on our land for over three hundred years. You took it from my people. You stole it from us. Now we are taking back what is rightfully ours.' No one said a word. 'But we do not want to live in your stinking hovels so we are going to burn the whole place down. By this evening it will be as if it never existed. That way you'll have nothing to come back to, will you?' Still no one said anything.

Sofia was screaming inside herself, 'Don't just stand there. Tell him he can't do it. Stop him. What's the matter with you all?'

'Now,' the cowboy soldier went on as he swaggered along the side of his tank. 'Here's what you do. The men, if you can call yourselves men, you get in those lorries outside the shop. Be good boys now. Off you go.' No one moved. He took out his pistol and pointed it at the doctor. 'Go,' he said quietly.

'Where are we going?' the doctor asked.

'You'll see,' replied the cowboy soldier.

Sofia ducked down. A soldier was walking towards the toilets. Sofia prayed, her eyes tight shut, fists and jaws clenched. 'Don't let him come in. Don't let him come in. Be good, God. Don't let him come in.'

He came in. She heard the tap running into the basin. He was drinking. Then he spoke, 'Forgive me,' he whispered. 'Dear God, forgive me. I begged the captain. I begged him, but he wouldn't listen. Rats, he said, they breed like rats. You burn rats out. You destroy them. But they're not rats, they're flesh and blood. Oh God, oh God.' He was sobbing and then he was kicking the wall. That was the moment Sofia shifted her weight on to her bad ankle and slipped. The sobbing stopped at once. Sofia shrank back as the footsteps came towards her. She could hear his breathing through the door.

'Whoever you are,' his voice was urgent but gentle, 'whoever's in there, just listen to me. Whatever happens, stay where you are. Believe me, where they're going, you don't want to go. Stay put. Don't move. I'll do what I can.' And then he was gone.

It was some time after he'd left before Sofia screwed up enough courage to look out of her window again.

When she did, she saw the last of the men from the village climbing up into the lorry. There were two lorry loads of them. A fierce anger welled up inside her. They were going like lambs, all of them. What of the rousing, triumphal songs they had sung so often in the café? What of Mr Kovacs' defiant exhortations that everyone must defend the homeland? How could they leave the women and the children without even a word of protest? How could they? The men were just sitting there with bowed heads, Mr Kovacs weeping openly. She hated him then even more than the cowboy soldier. She hated them all.

'Good,' said the cowboy soldier smiling. 'Good boys. Now, women and children to the other lorries, and don't worry yourselves, you'll all meet up again soon enough. Hurry now.' He waved his pistol, and the women and children drifted slowly, reluctantly, across to the other side of the square. The soldiers stood by and looked on as they struggled to clamber in. Only one of them stepped forward to pick up the smaller children and hand them up. Sofia wondered if it was her soldier. She hoped it was. He had long hair to his shoulders and a moustache like Father's. He seemed very young to be a soldier.

It took three of them to lift Mrs Marxova out of her wheelchair and up into the lorry. They were not gentle with her. One of them kicked away her chair so that it rolled down the road, hitting a curb and turning over in the gutter. They laughed at that. Mother helped Nan up into the lorry beside her and they sat down together, Nan's head resting on her shoulder. The lorries started up. Mother was calling for her now, crying.

Sofia made up her mind in that instant. She had to be with them. Why should she trust the soldier? She didn't even know him. She had hardly seen him. She unlocked the door and ran past the basins, forgetting her ankle. She slipped and fell by the doorway. By the time she was up on her feet again, she could hear the lorries already moving off. It was too late. Maybe, she thought, maybe the soldier was right after all. Maybe she was safer here, undiscovered. She hobbled back into the toilet and shut the door. She climbed up just in time to see the last lorry leaving the square and her mother's scarved head still turning, still looking. She was still crying.

The cowboy soldier leapt down off his tank. 'You know what to do. I don't want a building left standing. Understand? Nothing. You'll find all the petrol you need in the garage. Use hay, faggots, anything that'll burn. If it won't burn, then blow it up.' The soldiers cheered at that. Whooping and yelling, they scattered in all directions, some diving directly into the houses on the square and others running off down the village streets. Soon the square was left to the cowboy soldier who sat down on a bench and lit up another cigarette. He blew smoke rings into the air and poked his finger through them. Martha's dog was snuffling around her body, his tail between his legs.

Sofia could not look any more. She sat down. The blood had congealed on her leg. She took off her sock. Her ankle was puffed up and grey.

A window shattered somewhere in the village, then another, then another. Some way away, a gun began to chatter and did not stop.

'Are you still in there?' It was the soldier's voice from below her window.

'Yes,' she replied at once, without thinking.

'For God's sake, don't try to run. You'll be seen. They'll kill you if they see you. They mustn't leave any witnesses.'

'My mother, my nan. They were in the lorry. Where have you taken them? Where have they gone?'

'You don't want to know,' said the soldier. 'Just worry about yourself. And don't look out of the window. They'll see you. I could see the shape of your head from across the square. Keep down. I can't stay.' Sofia heard him walk away. She wanted to ask him so much more but could not risk calling out. She sat down on the toilet and tried to gather her thoughts, but nothing would come but tears. Racked with sobbing, Sofia put her head between her knees and hugged herself into a tight ball and closed her eyes. So she sat for hour after hour as they burnt the village around her. Trying not to listen, not to smell.

The first explosion was from far away, but all the same, it rocked the building, blasted her ears and left a ringing inside her head that would not stop. The next was closer, in the square itself, maybe the post office she thought, and the next shortly afterwards was even closer still. Perhaps the café. She bit her lip till it bled, determined not to scream, not to give herself away. When plaster crashed down from the ceiling on to her shoulders, she could stand it no longer. She lifted her head and screamed and screamed. Through her own screaming, through the whistle in her ears, she heard the whoosh and crackle of the flames outside, the roar of the roofs collapsing, and always the soldiers whooping.

Then she saw smoke drifting in under her door, thick smoke that would stifle the life out of her. She had to get away. She climbed up on to the seat and put her nose to the window to breathe in the last of the cleaner air. That was when the tanks began to fire from under the trees, pounding, pounding, pounding. She fell backwards on to the floor, back down into the smoke. She rolled into a corner, covering her face, her mouth, her ears, clenching herself into herself as tight as she would fit. Then she prayed. The picture she had seen on television of the child without any legs flashed into her head. 'Please God, I want my legs. I need my legs. Let me die if you want, but I want my legs. I want my legs.'

The smoke was thinning. Suddenly she could breathe without coughing, then there were voices outside.

'The toilets. Don't forget the toilets.' It was the cowboy soldier. 'A grenade will do it.'

'Hardly worth the trouble, Captain,' said another. Her soldier, her soldier's voice. 'It's not as if there's anyone left to piss in it, is there? And anyway, why don't we leave it there as a monument. All that's left of them, their toilet.'

The cowboy soldier laughed. 'Good. Very good. I like it. Some bonfire, eh?' They were walking away now. The cowboy soldier went on, 'D'you see the mosque come down? Obstinate beggar, he was. Took twenty rounds to topple him. This heat gives a man a thirst, eh? Let's get at the beer.'

'Why not,' said Sofia's soldier.

There were no more shootings after that, no more explosions, but Sofia stayed where she was, curled up on the floor of the toilet. She could hear the soldiers carousing in the square and the sound of smashing beer bottles. One crashed against the window above her head, shattering the glass. Shortly after, their laughter was drowned out by the noise of the tank engines starting up. They were calling each other. They were going. She waited a few minutes more until she was quite sure the tanks were on the move, their engines revving. Then she climbed up and looked out. The two tanks were rumbling away out of sight, belching black smoke out behind them. They were gone.

Everywhere she looked was utter destruction. The village was a flaming, smoking ruin. Like all the other buildings, the café had no roof. Flames licked out of the windows, leaping across the road into the trees. The parked cars were blackened shells now, the tyres still burning furiously. The front of the shop had entirely caved in. Sofia got down, opened the door and hobbled out into the square. The minaret had fallen right across School Lane, obliterating the houses beneath. Martha still lay outside her café, but now her dog was beside her. He was not moving. Sofia sat down on the bench in the middle of the square where she was farthest from the heat of the fires. She had no tears left to cry.

She was still sitting there late that evening when the reporters came in their Land Rover. She was rocking back and forth and there was a cow beside her, grazing the grass. She was humming 'Raining in My Heart'. She looked up at them as they approached.

'Hello,' she said. 'That's Myrtle. She's come to find me. She wants milking.'

'Is this your village?' asked a reporter, pushing a microphone at her. Sofia looked at him blankly. 'What does it feel like to see it like this?' he went on. 'And what do you think of the people who've done it? Where the hell is everyone, anyway?'

'I've got my legs,' said Sofia, and she smiled. 'I've got my legs. God is great.'

The Owl and the Pussycat

I'm a lucky fellow. I live in the wilds of North Devon,
in the same valley where Williamson set his wonderful
Tarka the Otter. *I have walked to work for over*
twenty years across fields, down country lanes. One
morning, on the way to milking, I discovered a tawny
owlet, grounded, helpless.

It was a summer morning in mist with sleep still in my
head. As I walked the long way down the lane to the
dairy I saw something strangely alive against the rigid
cold stones of the wall, but I was too detached to bother
about it. It was only as I was milking Herma, the cow
with the kick, that my mind finally emerged from the
shades of the night's rest. She stood eating her cake
while I washed her and dried her off, and I slipped the
cluster on easily. Like a statue she stood, her feet
planted in the concrete, while the milk gushed down

warm and white into the jar below. She milked out her regular four gallons and I bent to remove the cluster. It was her karate kick that woke me. As I touched the cluster, her leg flashed forward and sent it sprawling on the ground underneath her. I reached out to retrieve it. She shuffled like a heavyweight boxer and kicked out viciously, catching me across my wrist. Only then, as I cursed her, did I come to realise that the soft grey patch against the stone wall of the lane had been an owl. I would have a look later, I thought.

But as I finished the milking and drove the cows back out on to their silver-cobwebbed field, I remembered the great ginger tomcat that lived in and around the calf pens, not twenty yards from the spot where I had seen the owl. The yard could wait. I would wash down later. Still in the slippery rubber armour of the dairy I ran back up the lane, my waders squeaking against each other. I reached the place, or what I thought might have been the place, but there was no owl. I looked higher up the lane, shielding my eyes against the shafts of sunlight that filtered through the elms above. The great ginger tom looked down on me from the sun at the top of the garden wall, his tail whipping from side to side menacingly.

It was the cat that convinced me I had not been ng, and I looked now for the mangled, contorted mess of a murdered tawny owlet. I searched for fifty yards in both directions, on both sides of the lane. All the way along, the banks were six feet high above stone walls, too high to climb. And he was too small to fly. No sign anywhere – no feathers, no blood. The cat must have taken him off elsewhere for the kill. I glanced up to the top of the garden wall. The cat was still there, still swishing his tail at me.

On an impulse, perhaps it was resentment that he had got there first, I reached down, picked up a stone and threw it up towards the cat. The stone cracked and shattered against the wall, and the cat was gone, leaving me staring into the glare of the sun.

I undid my milking-apron and pulled it up over my head. As I threw it over my shoulder my hand must have slipped because the apron fell to the ground. That was the moment I saw him, a black eye blink against the stone, like the shutter of a camera. I bent to look more closely and there, exactly where I had first seen him, was the small tawny owlet with wisps for feathers. With both eyes now closed he had become part of the stone wall, part of a patchwork of wet, grey-brown stone and dank weeds. If his camouflage was imperfect, it was only that he was perhaps a more mottled stone than the other stones around him.

He came into my hands quietly submissive. There

was no panicky flapping of wings, no raucous shrieking as I gathered him up in both hands and cradled him against my chest. Thin and wet and weak, he could muster the energy only to blink his boot-black eyes. I ran my fingers under his claws in an effort to make him grasp me; but the claws lay limp and cold, curled up underneath him. His hook beak remained tight shut, locked down into his feathers. I thought briefly of leaving him where he was, of climbing the high elms above the lane to find his home. I thought too of bashing his head against a stone – weak as he was, he would have died more quickly than a trout. But then I thought of the ginger tom. If it was right to kill the bird, then why not let the cat kill him and have some profit from the kill? I confess now that I took the bird in, took him under my wing, so to speak, so that the cat should not have him.

I knew little enough about owls. I was aware they were meat eaters, and that they hunted at night. I had seen them often enough making low-flying sorties over the hedges at dusk. And at night, coming back across the moonlit fields from milking, I had heard them calling out across their dark kingdom, filling the night air with their stuttering cries that always seemed to end on the long falling note they first intended. But the closest I had been to an owl was in *Winnie the Pooh*, or with a pussycat riding the seas in a beautiful peagreen boat. Of course I could have asked. But then I would have had to have taken the advice offered, and that was difficult. Mother would have had it in the airing cupboard, feeding it on steak; and Father would have killed it there and then. A compromise would not have been easy, so I decided to do it my way.

The old shippen was the best place. All the stock were out to grass and no one ever came near the place in summer. I had cleaned it out only the week before. There were rats of course, but I hadn't seen any in there for months. I laid him down gently on a bed of hay in an empty water trough. He lay like a patient on his back, the only sign of life in his cold, tired body were those hypnotic, slow-winking eyes.

Worms seemed to me to be the right way to start, so I left him in the dark where he lay and went hunting. It is remarkable that worms seem to know when you are after them. Any afternoon digging the vegetable garden I would turn them up by the hundreds, but now when I needed them all I could manage in half an hour were half a dozen miserable, emaciated specimens. But I was anxious to get some food inside him.

At first he just blinked while I dangled one in front of him. I rubbed it gently against the point of his black beak, but it would not open. I tried setting him on his feet, thinking he might not like to feed lying on his back; but there was no strength in his legs and he would not grip with his claws. He toppled over and flapped his wings to right himself. I held him upright against me and pressed the worm against his beak. He blinked slowly, the shutters over his eyes coming down like those of a ventriloquist's dummy. Then with no warning the head turned sideways, the beak opened, reached out and took the worm. It proved to be an awkward worm, wrapping itself around his beak. But a shake or two of the head and it was gone. They eyes winked black again. He dealt with the remaining five worms with extreme efficiency but with an air of supercilious detachment that almost irritated me. I was pleased he was strong enough to eat, but my pleasure was overshadowed by the feeling that he was not in the slightest bit grateful for my mining efforts in the vegetable patch.

I fed him four times more that day, and by the evening he was standing huddled into the side of the trough, with his grey feathers turned tawny brown, fluffed out and dry. He would live now if I could keep him going.

After milking the next morning I went into the shippen with a tinful of lusciously wriggling worms –

one as long as a small snake. The water trough in the corner was empty. I shut the door quickly behind me, and turned on the light, but there was no sign of the owl at first. Had he not snapped his beak I doubt I would have found him at all. From the darkest corner of the shippen came the sound of irregular tapping, like wood against wood in short sharp bursts. He was wedged into the corner, his swivel-head turned around aiming at me; and all the while as I approached slowly he snapped his beak in agitation. I picked him up but his wings were stronger now, and he fought me for a moment or two in an effort to break free. I held him tight and set him back in his trough for his breakfast. This time there was no hesitation. Within a minute the tin was empty and he was clapping his beak at me for more.

All that day I fed him on worms, all day he ate everything I put in front of him. Father was beginning to wonder why I insisted on digging the vegetable patch every spare minute I had. It took too long and I knew I could no longer maintain the worm supply. It was the dog eating his dinner that night that gave me the idea of an alternative food source. Mother fed the dog on chunks of ox cheek every evening. No one would notice if a few ounces went missing every day.

I cut it up quite small to start with and the owl took

it from me with ever increasing enthusiasm. He clapped at me when I went in to feed him, he clapped at me in between mouthfuls, and he clapped at me when I went out. I could never make out whether this last clapping meant 'Goodbye', or 'Get out and find me some more.'

I looked up owls in the only book I could find. I read what I knew already but had not thought about: that an owl eats his prey whole, he doesn't fillet it, that his digestion needs the bone, the hair, the feathers. Accordingly, I wrapped the chunks of meat in duck feathers before I fed them to him. Any mice the cats brought in I pounced on and took out to him. I even cornered a little fieldmouse myself, but held my hand at the last moment. He ate everything; he left nothing behind. Within a few days I picked up an owl pellet from the floor under the trough.

He had taken to perching now, and was making flying sallies across the shippen from one hayrack to the other. Sometimes he would misjudge the height and overestimate his own flight capabilities, and he would hit the hayrack too low and fall back on to the floor. Then he would flutter shame-faced into a corner and clap his anger and frustration at me. He had now become difficult to feed, striking often at my finger as much as at the food I held out to him. I took to wearing a gardening glove for self-protection.

All the time he grew. His wisps turned to full brown feathers, the face took on the predatory look of a grown owl with dark rings encircling the great shining eyes. I could feel through my glove the power and killing potential of his claws.

For some days more he was willing to come on to my hand to eat the food I brought him, but then one morning I found he would no longer come near me. If approached, he would fly away, and if I cornered him in the trough or in one of his brooding corners, he would strike at me like a cobra as I offered the meat, clapping his beak and flashing his eyes in fury. I was offended, yet pleased he had relearnt the aggression he would need if he was to survive outside the sanctuary of the shippen.

My plan was to release him when I was satisfied he could feed himself, and when he no longer made any flying errors, but it would be some time before he could kill for himself. Morning and evening now I placed his food along the top of the high hayrack. He glared at me from a distance, following me with his periscope head until I was gone. I used to spy on him through a hole in the door. Within minutes he would fly up to the hayrack and take the food, tearing it into manageable pieces between his claws and his beak. He was ready to fly. The hayrack was the perfect place to leave food, high and inaccessible to anything without wings. He had come to accept that this was his dining area, and providing I kept replenishing the stocks he would survive.

That last evening, after I had put out his meat I went out leaving open the upper door of the shippen. The last I saw of him, he was sitting at the other end of the hayrack from his food, waiting for me to go so he could eat his meat in peace. I wished him good luck and left.

Next morning the food was gone, and so was the owl. I looked in all his dark corners, along all the hayracks. He was gone. No one clapped at me when I left. That evening, before dark, I lined his meat up along the hayrack, leaving the upper stable door open so that he could fly in. I waited as long as I could to see if he would come for it. He never came, but I had the feeling that he was watching me from the branches of the elms around the yard.

First thing the next morning before milking I checked the hayrack in the shippen. The meat was gone. The owl had taken it. Every bit was gone. My plan had worked. How I sang in the dairy that morning.

For ten days or more I replaced the food in the shippen, and every morning it was gone. Once, late in the evening when I was checking a cow due to calve, I fancied I caught a glimpse of the slow silent flight of an owl out of the great beech tree by the pond, but I could not be sure it was him.

It was at breakfast that Father spoke of it first. 'Forgot to tell you,' he said, pulling up his chair. 'I found a dead owl yesterday down the lane by the parlour. Just by the gate. He was as thin as a rake. Starved to death I shouldn't wonder.'

'Rejected by the parents,' said Mother. 'They do that you know.'

'Tawny owl?' I said, hoping against hope.

'Think so – young one too, I'd say.'

'Where is he?' I asked, trying to sound only mildly interested.

'I left him where he was,' my father said.

I ran out of the house and down the lane under the avenue of elms, past the place where I had first found him. He lay spread-eagled by the gateway, his dead black eyes no longer shining. His beak was half open; all dignity, all power gone.

I buried him in the spinney under the elms he was born in. He was stiff and cold and I could not cover him quickly enough.

That night, under the stars, I waited by the shippen with my gun. The meat was lined up on the hayrack, as usual. I did not have long to wait. The cat came in under the fence from the field, padding gently across the cobbles, sidestepping the puddles. Easily he leapt the door. By the time I got there, silent as a man can be, the great ginger tom was at his evening meal up on the hayrack. I fired both barrels at him and saw him fall before I turned away and went back home.

Muck and Magic

(For Elisabeth Frink)

Some years ago, we got to know Elisabeth Frink, a wonderful sculptor, particularly of horses, and a kind and generous person too. She became a great friend and ally in life. Sadly, she died all too young. Her very last work now hangs above the west door of Liverpool Cathedral. It is a Risen Christ.

I am sometimes asked these days how I got started. I should love to be able to say that it was all because I had some dream, some vision, or maybe that I just studied very hard. None of this would really be true. I owe what I am, what I have become, what I do each day of my life, to a bicycle ride I took a long time ago now, when I was twelve years old – and also to a pile of muck, horse muck.

The bike was new that Christmas. It was maroon, and I remember it was called a Raleigh Wayfarer. It had all you could ever dream of in a bike – in those days. It had a bell, a dynamo lamp front and rear, five gears and a silver pump. I loved it instantly and spent every hour I could out riding it. And when I wasn't riding it, I was polishing it.

We lived on the edge of town, so it was easy to ride off down Mill Lane past the estate, along the back of the soap factory where my father worked, and then out into the countryside beyond. How I loved it. In a car, you zoomed past so fast that the cows and the trees were only ever brief, blurred memories. On my bike I was close to everything for the first time. I felt the cold and the rain on my face. I mooed at the cows, and they looked up and blinked at me lazily. I shouted at the crows and watched them lift off cawing and croaking into the wind. But best of all, no one knew where I was – and that included me sometimes. I was always getting myself lost and coming back at dusk, late. I would brace myself for all the sighing and tutting and ticking off that inevitably followed. I bore it all stoically because they didn't really mean it, and anyway it had all been worth it. I'd had a taste of real freedom and I wanted more of it.

After a while I discovered a circuit that seemed to be just about ideal. It was a two-hour run, not too many hills going up, plenty going down, a winding country lane that criss-crossed a river past narrow cottages where hardly anyone seemed to live, under the shadow of a church where sometimes I stopped and put flowers on the graves that everyone else seemed to have forgotten, and then along the three-barred iron fence where the horses always galloped over to see me, their tails and heads high, their ears pricked.

There were three of them: a massive bay hunter that looked down on me from a great height, a chubby little pony with a face like a chipmunk, and a fine-boned grey that flowed and floated over the ground with such grace and ease that I felt like clapping every time I saw her move. She made me laugh too because she often made rude, farty noises as she came trotting over to see me. I called her Peg after a flying horse called Pegasus that I'd read about in a book. The small one I called Chip, and the great bay, Big Boy. I'd cuddle them all, give each of them a sugar lump – two for Peg because she wasn't as pushy as the other two – told them my troubles, cuddled them a little more and went on my way, always reluctantly.

I hated to leave them because I was on the way back home after that, back to homework, and the sameness of the house, and my mother's harassed scurrying and my little brother's endless tantrums. I lay in my room and dreamed of those horses, of Peg in particular.

I pictured myself riding her bareback through flowery meadows, up rutty mountain passes, fording rushing streams where she'd stop to drink. I'd go to sleep at nights lying down on the straw with her, my head resting on her warm belly. But when I woke, her belly was always my pillow, and my father was in the bathroom next door, gargling and spitting into the sink, and there was school to face, again. But after school I'd be off on my bike and that was all that mattered to me. I gave up ballet lessons on Tuesdays. I gave up cello lessons Fridays. I never missed a single day, no matter what the weather – rain, sleet, hail – I simply rode through it all, living for the moment when Peg would rest her heavy head on my shoulder and I'd hear that sugar lump crunching inside her great grinding jaw.

It was spring. I know that because there were daffodils all along the grass verge by the fence, and there was nowhere to lie my bike down on the ground without squashing them. So I leaned it up against the fence and fished in my pocket for the sugar lumps. Chip came scampering over as he always did, and Big Boy wandered lazily up behind him, his tail flicking nonchalantly. But I saw no sign of Peg. When Big Boy had finished his sugar lump, he started chewing at the saddle of my bike and knocked it over. I was just picking it up when I saw her coming across the field towards me. She wore long green boots and a jersey covered in planets and stars, gold against the dark, deep blue of space. But what struck me most was her hair, the wild white curly mop of it, around her face that was somehow both old and young at the same time.

'Who are you?' she asked. It was just a straight question, not a challenge.

'Bonnie,' I replied.

'She's not here,' said the woman.

'Where is she?'

'It's the spring grass. I have to keep her inside from now on.'

'Why?'

'Laminitis. She's fine all through the winter, eats all the grass she likes no trouble. But she's only got to sniff the spring grass and it comes back. It heats the hoof, makes her lame.' She waved away the two horses and came closer, scrutinising me. 'I've seen you before, haven't I? You like horses, don't you?' I smiled. 'Me too,' she went on. 'But they're a lot of work.'

'Work?' I didn't understand.

'Bring them in, put them out, groom them, pick out their feet, feed them, muck them out. I'm not as young as I was, Bonnie. You don't want a job do you, in the stables? Be a big help. The grey needs a good long walk every day, and a good mucking out. Three pounds an hour, what do you say?'

Just like that. I said yes, of course. I could come evenings and weekends.

'I'll see you tomorrow then,' she said. 'You'll need wellies. I've got some that should fit. You be careful on the roads now.' And she turned and walked away.

I cycled home that day singing my heart out and high as a kite. It was my first paying job, and I'd be looking after Peg. It really was a dream come true.

I didn't tell anyone at home, nor at school. Where I went on my bike, what I did, was my own business, no one else's. Besides there was always the chance that father would stop me – you never knew with him. And I certainly didn't want any of my school friends oaring in on this. At least two of them knew all about horses, or they said they did, and I knew they would never stop telling me the right way to do this or that. Best just to keep everything to myself.

To get to the house the next day – you couldn't see it from the road – I cycled up a long drive through high trees that whispered at me. I had to weave around the pot-holes, bump over sleeping policemen, but then came out on to a smooth tarmac lane where I could freewheel downhill and hear the comforting tic-a-tic of my wheels beneath me.

I nearly came off when I first saw them. Everywhere in amongst the trees there were animals, but none of them moved. They just looked at me. There were wild boar, dogs, horses, and gigantic men running through trees like hunters. But all were as still as statues. They *were* statues. Then I saw the stables on my right, Peg looking out at me, ears pricked and shaking her mane. Beyond the stables was a long house of flint and brick with a tiled roof, and a clock tower with doves fluttering around it.

The stable block was deserted. I didn't like to call out, so I opened the gate and went over to Peg and stroked her nose. That was when I noticed a pair of wellies waiting by the door, and slipped into one of them was a piece of paper. I took it out and read:

> *Hope these fit. Take her for a walk down the tracks, not in the fields. She can nibble the grass, but not too much. Then muck out the stables. Save what dry straw you can – it's expensive. When you've done, shake out half a bale in her stable – you'll find straw and hay in the barn. She has two slices of hay in her rack. Don't forget to fill up the water buckets.*

It was not signed.

Until then I had not given it a single thought, but I

had never led a horse or ridden a horse in all my life. Come to that, I hadn't mucked out a stable either. Peg had a halter on her already, and a rope hung from a hook beside the stable. I put the wellies on – they were only a little too big – clipped on the rope, opened the stable door and led her out, hoping, praying she would behave. I need not have worried. It was Peg that took me for a walk. I simply stopped whenever she did, let her nibble for a while, and then asked her gently if it wasn't time to move on. She knew the way, up the track through the woods, past the running men and the wild boar, then forking off down past the ponds where a bronze water buffalo drank without ever moving his lips. White fish glided ghostly under the shadow of his nose. The path led upwards from there, past a hen house where a solitary goose stretched his neck, flapped his wings and honked at us. Peg stopped for a moment, lifted her nose and wrinkled it at the goose who began preening himself busily. After a while I found myself coming back to the stable-yard gate and Peg led me in. I tied her up in the yard and set about mucking out the stables.

I was emptying the wheelbarrow on to the muck heap when I felt someone behind me. I turned round. She was older than I remembered her, greyer in the face, and more frail. She was dressed in jeans and a rough sweater this time, and seemed to be covered in white powder, as if someone had thrown flour at her. Even her cheeks were smudged with it. She glowed when she smiled.

'Where there's muck there's money, that's what they say,' she laughed; and then she shook her head. 'Not true, I'm afraid, Bonnie. Where there's muck, there's magic. Now that's true.' I wasn't sure what she meant by that. 'Horse muck,' she went on by way of explanation. 'Best magic in the world for vegetables. I've got leeks in my garden longer than, longer than . . .' She looked around her. 'Twice as long as your bicycle pump. All the soil asks is that we feed it with that stuff, and it'll do anything we want it to. It's like anything, Bonnie, you have to put in more than you take out. You want some tea when you've finished?'

'Yes please.'

'Come up to the house then. You can have your money.' She laughed at that. 'Maybe there is money in muck after all.'

As I watched her walk away, a small yappy dog came bustling across the lawn, ran at her and sprang into her arms. She cradled him, put him over her shoulder and disappeared into the house.

I finished mucking out the stable as quickly as I could, shook out some fresh straw, filled up the water buckets and led Peg back in. I gave her a goodbye kiss on the nose and rode my bike up to the house.

I found her in the kitchen, cutting bread.

'I've got peanut butter or honey,' she said. I didn't like either, but I didn't say so.

'Honey,' I said. She carried the mugs of tea, and I carried the plate of sandwiches. I followed her out across a cobbled courtyard, accompanied by the yappy dog, down some steps and into a great glass building where there stood a gigantic white horse. The floor was covered in newspaper, and everywhere was crunchy underfoot with plaster. The shelves all around were full of sculpted heads and arms and legs and hands. A white sculpture of a dog stood guard over the plate of sandwiches and never even sniffed them. She sipped her tea between her hands and looked up at the giant horse. The horse looked just like Peg, only a lot bigger.

'It's no good,' she sighed. 'She needs a rider.' She turned to me suddenly. 'You wouldn't be the rider, would you?' she asked.

'I can't ride.'

'You wouldn't have to, not really. You'd just sit there, that's all, and I'd sketch you.'

'What, now?'

'Why not? After tea be all right?'

And so I found myself sitting astride Peg that same afternoon in the stable yard. She was tied up by her rope, pulling contentedly at her hay net and paying no attention to us whatsoever. It felt strange up there, with Peg shifting warm underneath me. There was no saddle, and she asked me to hold the reins one-handed, loosely, to feel 'I was part of the horse'. The worst of it was that I was hot, stifling hot, because she had dressed me up as an Arab. I had great swathes of cloth over and around my head and I was draped to my feet with a long heavy robe so that nothing could be seen of my jeans or sweater or wellies.

'I never told you my name, did I?' said the lady, sketching furiously on a huge pad. 'That was rude of me. I'm Liza. When you come tomorrow, you can give me a hand making you if you like. I'm not as strong as I was, and I'm in a hurry to get on with this. You can mix the plaster for me. Would you like that?' Peg snorted and pawed the ground. 'I'll take that as a yes, shall I?' She laughed, and walked round behind the horse, turning the page of her sketch pad. 'I want to do one more from this side and one from the front, then you can go home.'

Half an hour later when she let me down and unwrapped me, my bottom was stiff and sore.

'Can I see?' I asked her.

'I'll show you tomorrow,' she said. 'You will come, won't you?' She knew I would, and I did.

I came every day after that to muck out the stables and to walk Peg, but what I looked forward to most – even more than being with Peg – was mixing up Liza's plaster for her in the bucket, climbing the stepladder with it, watching her lay the strips of cloth dunked in the wet plaster over the frame of the rider, building me up from the iron skeleton of wire, to what looked at first like an Egyptian mummy, then a riding Arab at one with his horse, his robes shrouding him with mystery. I knew all the while it was me in that skeleton, me inside that mummy. I was the Arab sitting astride his horse looking out over the desert. She worked ceaselessly, and with such a fierce determination that I didn't like to interrupt. We were joined together by a common, comfortable silence.

At the end of a month or so we stood back, the two of us, and looked up at the horse and rider, finished.

'Well,' said Liza, her hands on her hips. 'What do you think, Bonnie?'

'I wish,' I whispered, touching the tail of the horse, 'I just wish I could do it.'

'But you did do it, Bonnie,' she said and I felt her hand on my shoulder. 'We did it together. I couldn't have done it without you.' She was a little breathless as she spoke. 'Without you, that horse would never have had a rider. I'd never have thought of it. Without you mixing my plaster, holding the bucket, I couldn't have done it.' Her hand gripped me tighter. 'Do you want to do one of your own?'

'I can't.'

'Of course you can. But you have to look around you first, not just glance, but really look. You have to breathe it in, become a part of it, feel that you're a part of it. You draw what you see, what you feel. Then you make what you've drawn. Use clay if you like, or do what I do and build up plaster over a wire frame. Then set to work with your chisel, just like I do, until it's how you want it. If I can do it, you can do it. I tell you what. You can have a corner of my studio if you like, just so long as you don't talk when I'm working. How's that?'

So my joyous spring blossomed into a wonderful summer. After a while, I even dared to ride Peg bareback sometimes on the way back to the stable yard; and I never forgot what Liza told me. I looked about me. I listened. And the more I listened and the more I looked, the more I felt at home in this new world. I became a creature of the place. I belonged there as much as the wren that sang at me high on the vegetable garden wall, as much as the green dragonfly hovering over the pool by the water buffalo. I sketched Peg. I sketched Big Boy (I couldn't sketch Chip – he just came out round). I bent my wire frames into shape and

I began to build my first horse sculpture, layer on layer of strips of cloth dunked in plaster just like Liza did. I moulded them into shape on the frame, and when they dried I chipped away and sanded. But I was never happy with what I'd done.

All this time, Liza worked on beside me in the studio, and harder, faster, more intensely than ever. I helped her whenever she asked me, too, mixing, holding the bucket for her, just as I had done before.

It was a Rising Christ, she said, Christ rising from the dead, his face strong, yet gentle too, immortal it seemed; but his body, vulnerable and mortal. From time to time she'd come over and look at my stumpy effort that looked as much like a dog as a horse to me, and she would walk round it nodding her approval. 'Coming on, coming on,' she'd say. 'Maybe just a little bit off here perhaps.' And she'd chisel away for a minute or two, and a neck or leg would come to sudden life.

I told her once, 'Its like magic.'

She thought for a moment, and said, 'That's exactly what it is, Bonnie. It's a God-given thing, a God-given magic, and it's not to be wasted. Don't waste it, Bonnie. Don't ever waste it.'

The horse and rider came back from the foundry, bronze now and magnificent. I marvelled at it. It stood outside her studio, and when it caught the red of the evening sun, I could scarcely take my eyes off it. But these days Liza seemed to tire more easily, and she would sit longer over her tea, gazing out at her horse and rider.

'I am so pleased with that, Bonnie,' she said, 'so pleased we did it together.'

The Christ figure was finished and went off to the foundry a few weeks before I had to go on my summer holiday. 'By the time you come back again,' said Liza, 'it should be back. It's going to hang above the door of the village church. Isn't that nice? It'll be there for ever. Well, not for ever. Nothing is for ever.'

The holiday was in Cornwall. We stayed where we always did, in Cadgwith, and I drew every day. I drew boats and gulls and lobster pots. I made sculptures with wet sand – sleeping giants, turtles, whales – and everyone thought I was mad not to go swimming and boating. The sun shone for fourteen days. I never had such a perfect holiday, even though I didn't have my bike, or Peg or Liza with me.

My first day back, the day before school began, I cycled out to Liza's place with my best boat drawing in a stiff envelope under my sweater. The stable yard was deserted. There were no horses in the fields. Peg wasn't in her stable and I could find no one up at the house, no Liza, no yappy dog. I stopped in the village to ask but there was no one about. It was like a ghost village. Then the church bell began to ring. I leant my bike up against the churchyard wall and ran up the path. There was Liza's Rising Christ glowing in the sun above the doorway, and inside they were singing hymns.

I crept in, lifting the latch carefully so that I wouldn't be noticed. The hymn was just finishing. Everyone was sitting down and coughing. I managed to squeeze myself in at the end of a pew and sat down too. The church was packed. A choir in red robes and white surplices sat on either side of the altar. The vicar was taking off his glasses and putting them away. I looked everywhere for Liza's wild white curls, but could not find her. It was difficult for me to see much over everyone's heads. Besides, some people were wearing hats, so I presumed she was too and stopped looking for her. She'd be there somewhere.

The vicar began. 'Today was to be a great day, a happy day for all of us. Liza was to unveil her Rising Christ above the south door. It was her gift to us, to all of us who live here, and to everyone who will come here to our church in the centuries to come. Well, as we all now know, there was no unveiling, because she wasn't here to do it. On Monday evening last she watched her Rising Christ winched into place. She died the next day.'

I didn't hear anything else he said. It was only then that I saw the coffin resting on trestles between the pulpit and the lectern, with a single wreath of white flowers laid on it, only then that I took in the awful truth.

I didn't cry as the coffin passed right by me on its way out of the church. I suppose I was still trying to believe it. I stood and listened to the last prayers over the grave, numb inside, grieving as I had never grieved before, or since, but still not crying. I waited until almost everyone had gone and went over to the grave. A man was taking off his jacket and hanging it on the branch of the tree. He spat on his hands, rubbed them and picked up his spade. He saw me. 'You family?' he said.

'Sort of,' I replied. I reached inside my sweater and pulled out the boat drawing from Cadgwith. 'Can you put it in?' I asked. 'It's a drawing. It's for Liza.'

'Course,' he said, and he took it from me. 'She'd like that. Fine lady, she was. The things she did with her hands. Magic, pure magic.'

It was just before Christmas the same year that a cardboard tube arrived in the post, addressed to me. I opened it in the secrecy of my room. A rolled letter fell out, typed and very short.

Dear Miss Mallet,

 In her will, the late Liza Bonallack instructed us,
her solicitors, to send you this drawing. We would
ask you to keep us informed of any future changes of
address.

    With best wishes.

I unrolled it and spread it out. It was of me sitting on
Peg, swathed in Arab clothes. Underneath was written.

 For dearest Bonnie,

 I never paid you for all that mucking out, did I?
You shall have this instead, and when you are
twenty-one you shall have the artist's copy of our
horse and rider sculpture. But by then you will be
doing your own sculptures. I know you will.

    God bless,

    Liza.

So here I am, nearly thirty now. And as I look out at
the settling snow from my studio, I see Liza's horse and
rider standing in my back garden, and all around, my
own sculptures gathered in silent homage.

Silver Ghost

There are very few grand houses where I live, but I did hear of one. So I went to have a look.

The parkland was rolling and gracious, the driveway imposing, but at first glance I could see no house. Then I discovered there was no house, not any more. All I found was a plaque on a wall telling me the house had been destroyed by fire. No one knows how or why the fire started. Until now.

At about six o'clock on the evening of November 14th, 1969, a young man came into the pub at Nethercott Cross and asked for a beer. He took it away to a corner table by the fire and began to write feverishly in a notebook. When the landlord crouched down beside him to unload an armful of logs, he scarcely looked up, so engrossed was he in his writing. After some time he shut his notebook, sat back in his chair and sipped his drink, gazing into the fire. The pub cat jumped up on to his lap. 'So you recognise me too, do you?' he said, laughingly.

'Should he?' said the landlord from the bar.

'Well, Mr Glanville recognised me, up at Nethercott.'

'Mr Glanville?'

'He said I looked just like one of the portraits up there – "spitting image" he called it – and I did too. He showed me. The one in the Justice Room – it was like looking in a mirror.'

The landlord was puzzled. 'Who are you? Where you from?'

'Nat. Nathaniel Bickford,' replied the young man. 'I'm from Vermont, in the US. I've been looking for my English roots. My folks lived up at Nethercott – way, way back, hundred years or more. What a place! And the things that old Mr Glanville told me. Quite a story.'

'Percy Glanville?' said the landlord. 'Little bent sort of fellow? Silvery hair? Old as the hills?'

'That's the guy,' said Nat.

The landlord stood for a moment, frowning. 'So he's home again then, is he?' he said at last. 'I thought the old boy was still in hospital. Got a dicky heart. Well, I expect I'll be seeing him soon then. He spends half his life in here – not that I'm complaining, mind. But between you and me, he drinks too much. He writes poetry too. Bit of a strange one, if you know what I mean.'

That was the last time they spoke. Nathaniel

Bickford, an aspiring poet himself, decided he didn't like the landlord. He stood with his back against the fire and drank his beer down quickly. He wrapped his multicoloured scarf round his neck, picked up his rucksack and walked out into the darkness.

Later, the landlord would recall every word that had passed between them. He would remember the rainbow-coloured scarf, the young man's American accent, his height – about six foot one – his long, fair hair with a band round it like tennis players wear, and the exact time the young man had left. He told the police: 'I'd say he stayed for about half an hour, no more. So he must have left just after six-thirty.'

At half-past seven that same evening, Gabriel Penberthy, who grazed his sheep on the parkland around Nethercott House, looked out of his bathroom window at home. He noticed that every light up in the house seemed to be on and he thought that was strange, because no one lived there. The place was due to be opened to the public in a week. There was some plumbing work still being done, but he remembered seeing the plumber's van rattling off down the drive at dusk. No one else should have been up there. Gabriel Penberthy pulled aside the net curtain, opened the window and looked out. Then he saw that the lights were not lights at all but flickering flames. The house was ablaze from end to end. He could see smoke now, rising black into the moonlit night and sparks were funnelling up from the chimney stacks.

It was Gabriel Penberthy who called the fire brigade. The fire engines came from Holsworthy, Torrington and Hatherleigh. But they were too late and too few. Nothing could be done.

Meanwhile Nathaniel Bickford had at last hitched a ride back into Hatherleigh in a smelly Land Rover with a calf in the back. The driver sniffed and wiped his nose with his sleeve, eyed Nat with suspicion but said nothing all the way there. Back in his bedroom at The George, Nat had a deep and steaming bath, and shivered the cold out of him. Afterwards he lay on his bed and read through the notes he'd made back at the pub at Nethercott Cross. The extraordinary events of the day and the old man's story had set his mind racing. He decided to write it down right away so that he lost none of the detail of it, so that it was fresh in his head. He sat propped up against a pile of pillows, put his diary against his knees and the notebook on the bed beside him and began to write.

November 18th
I have walked today the soil my ancestors walked a hundred years ago. I have sat in the chairs my ancestors

sat in a hundred years ago. I have stretched out on their beds. I have rummaged through their cellars. In my rucksack I have a handful of ancestral acorns and I shall plant them back home in Vermont. They'll grow roots in Spring Farm soil just as my family did a century ago. Mission accomplished. Roots discovered. But roots wasn't all I discovered today. In the process I came up with something a whole lot more interesting.

This is my second night at The George – very quaint and olde England: thatched roof, oak beams to hit your head on, and genuine cobwebs from the sixteenth century. And beer! Last night I drank a lot of their warm beer, too much. Why do I always drink too much? I managed to struggle out this morning in time for a late breakfast – bacon and eggs and sausages. No maple syrup, no waffles, but breakfast is about the best thing the Brits do when it comes to food. I thumbed a ride through a kind of marshy, dank wasteland and found myself at Nethercott house – the 'family seat' – at about noon. Some guy in a tractor dropped me at the end of the drive, said I had a long walk ahead of me, and that there'd like as not be no one up there in the house to let me in. Gloomy kind of a guy, lugubrious. He turned out to be right. It was a long way up that drive, but the sight of Nethercott House standing proud, looking down over its wonderful rolling parkland, beckoned me on.

Some might think it a plain sort of a house, brick-built, symmetrical, a bit severe perhaps. But it suits the place. It fits in the landscape just like it grew there. Not large enough to dominate, not small enough to be ignored, it simply belongs. I had to keep reminding myself as I walked up the drive. This is really it! This is where the Bickfords come from. This is my place. And the lugubrious guy on the tractor was proved right again. Except for an old pick-up truck parked at the side of the house there was no one about.

The house was bathed in cold autumn sunlight and there was a stillness over the place that made it all seem unreal. Only the sheep moved, scattering when I came near and looking at me with accusing eyes, wishing me away. The flock drifted into the valley, bleating balefully at me. I bleated right back and laughed aloud at them. That was when I happened to glance up at the house. I saw a face in an attic window, hands flat on the windowpane either side of it, a face that fixed me with a look so hostile that I hesitated about venturing any nearer. Hell no, I thought, I've come all this way across the Atlantic to see this place. I'm not letting a pair of eyes scare me off. I waved cheerily at the face and it vanished at once. I walked on, steeling myself.

It was some minutes later that I first heard the knocking, metal on metal or wood on metal. I couldn't be sure which. It came not from the house itself, but from the woods behind and beyond. I passed alongside a high stone garden wall, the knocking so regular that I thought it must be mechanical. Through the trees I glimpsed open garage doors; and inside, a large car shrouded in a white sheet. The knocking had stopped, and then out of the hollow silence came a man's voice, and none too friendly.

'Give us a hand here, will you?' The man wasn't just old, he was ancient. He had a mallet in his hand. The gas tank beside him was covered in ivy.

'Beggering tap's stuck again,' he said. 'You have a go.'

The tap moved at the second blow and came free at the next. The gas poured out into the can below, splashing over my feet. I stepped back quickly and almost tripped. The old man had me by the elbow and steadied me. 'We'll wipe it off inside,' he said and turned off the tap. When he turned round he was beaming at me. He took off his flat cap and held out a shaky hand. 'I'm Percy Glanville,' he said. 'I live here. This is my place.' The old man's hand was cold in mine. His face was shrunken and shrivelled with age. There was a grey pallor in his cheeks, and his eyes were bloodshot, as if he had not slept for a year. His coat – a khaki military coat – had no buttons and was tied around his waist with string. The only thing clean about him was his silver hair.

'Is it your car?' I asked him. I was curious to know what was under the covers.

'Oh yes. She's mine.' His eyes twinkled with excitement. 'You want to see her?'

'She looks like a ghost under that sheet,' I said.

'Funny you should say that,' he chuckled, and he took hold of the sheet. 'Close your eyes. Go on . . . now you can open them.' The car shimmered silver in the sunlight. It shone so brightly that my eyes hurt and I had to turn away.

'Well?' The old man was at my shoulder.

'It's magnificent,' I said, running my hand along her cold bonnet. 'Old Rolls-Royce, isn't it?'

'1921 Rolls-Royce. Silver Ghost. Park Ward body. We had her from new. She's only done 21,000 miles in forty-eight years, and I drove every one of them myself. That's the best car in the world you're looking at, and she's mine. Worth a fortune too, but I'd never sell her. You want to see inside her?' He never waited for a reply. He showed me over the engine, which was as highly polished as the rest. He told me how he had only recently ground down the pistons. Every detail of the car was a marvel to him, from the red badge on the radiator, to the walnut dash, to the matching suitcases in the carpeted boot. I never knew that anyone could love a car so much.

'She needs petrol,' he said, unscrewing the cap. 'Be a good lad and pour it for me, will you?' It was a moment or two before I remembered that 'petrol' was gas. I used a funnel, but the can was awkward and the angle wrong, so that by the time I had finished, my trousers were spattered with gas.

'We'll put her to bed and then we'll have a cup of tea, shall we?' said the old man. And between us we draped the Silver Ghost in her sheet, closed the garage doors and left her there in the dark.

He lived next to the garage. It was a dingy place, and there was an all-pervading stench of drink and cats. The cats, perhaps a dozen of them, came yowling round us. The room was strewn with scraps of paper, written on and discarded; and everywhere there were books, and bottles – empty whisky bottles.

He talked at me from the kitchen, suddenly full of questions. Who was I? What was I doing here? But I had the feeling either that he wasn't interested in my answers or that he knew the answers already – how, I could not imagine.

It unnerved me, but I told him just the same, about how the family had left Nethercott a hundred years before to go sheep farming in Vermont, how we don't keep sheep any more, just maple trees for syrup and Jersey cows for milk and how I'd always wanted to come back and find my English roots. I sat smothered in cats, sipping hot, sweet tea, and in the intermittent silences, thumbing through a much-used copy of Longfellow's poems that I'd found on the table in front of me. As he sat down in the chair opposite me, I told him about the face I'd seen in the attic window. He didn't seem to hear. So I asked again, louder. Still no answer. He stirred his tea slowly. I tried another question. 'Who does Nethercott belong to now?' I asked.

When he looked up at me his eyes had turned suddenly cold and hard. 'You ask too many questions,' he said, an edge to his voice. 'But if you must know, the house belongs to me. Everything here belongs to me, the car, the house, everything. I worked for it, didn't I? I'm not like your kind. I was born with nothing, nothing but a name. No roots to go looking for. No ancestors. No stones to mark where we are. When we're alive no one cares. When we're gone no one cares.'

He sat back in his chair, nursing his mug of tea in his lap. 'I've got nothing to hide, nothing to be ashamed of. I'm over ninety. I was in the war, the Great War – 1914–18. Bengie was a young lieutenant, eighteen, hardly shaving. If you're a Bickford, then he'd be a cousin of yours, I suppose. I was his batman, servant if you like. Same age as he was. Like brothers we were, looked out for each other. Somehow we lived through it all and he brought me back here to be his farm manager and to look after him. He bought the Silver Ghost new in 1921. "If I die," he says, "the car's yours." He was always talking about dying. He had the gas in the war – weak lungs. He was never really well after that.

'Thirty years near enough, we lived here, happy as you like. Bit of a poet he was, but his eyes weren't too good, so I'd read to him and that way I became a bit of a poet myself – still am. We did everything together, him and me. We went fishing, hunting, played cards. Sometimes we'd just sit and talk for hours on end. He always told me, "I've got no one else to leave the place to, Percy, so I'm leaving it all to you." And I believed him. I believed him!'

He shook his head and wiped his watery eyes. Then he went on. 'If he ever wanted to go anywhere, and it wasn't often, I'd drive him. He loved that car as much as I do. We looked after her together. No mechanics, just him and me. Then one day I goes to fetch him from the station in the car and he's got this . . . woman with him. Helen May Lasky. He's met her at the races and he's gone and married her. He never asks me, mind you, just goes ahead and does it. And would I mind going and living in the stables? Would I mind! Oh, they made it nice enough for me – inside bathroom, electrics, and I had the Silver Ghost to talk to next door.'

As he talked now, the tears were running down his cheeks into the corners of his mouth. 'I wouldn't have minded, but she was always so high and mighty with me. I never hated anyone as much, not even the Germans I fought in the trenches, no one. She felt just the same about me too, and she didn't trouble to hide it either. She said I wasn't to call him Bengie, like I always had. I had to call him "Sir", and I had to call her "Madam". I could see Bengie hated it, but he would never argue with her, never. He was sick with love for her, bewitched he was. Can't think why. She never looked after him like she should have. She was always letting him catch chills. I warned her. I warned her. I told her times he wasn't to get cold and wet else he'd have his chest trouble again. She wouldn't listen. She knew best.

'So she goes fishing with him, early in the season, March it was and driving wind and rain. He comes back looking like death. He knew it was the finish of him. He told me I had to promise to look after her, so what else could I do? He was dead by the summer, twenty years ago last June. I sprinkled his ashes on the croquet lawn, and she watches from the window because it's raining. We liked croquet, Bengie and me. Nothing better on a summer's evening. But Bengie lied to me. He left everything to her. Oh, I had my cottage for my lifetime, but everything else – the car, the house, everything he'd promised me, he left to her. And that's not the half of it. She calls me in the day after I'd spread his ashes. She wants to buy me off. She'll pay me a thousand pounds if I leave the cottage tomorrow. I was tempted, I can tell you. But I didn't want to live anywhere else. And besides, I'd promised Bengie, hadn't I? So I stayed, and it was a good thing for her that I did.

'She wouldn't listen now any more than when Bengie was alive. She wasted all the money Bengie had left her on breeding horses that ran fast as the wind in her head but slow as carthorses on the racing tracks. The money was running out. The cook had to leave, then the housemaids, then the farm labourers. In the end there was just me – cook, butler, stable lad, chauffeur and shepherd, all in one. And never a kind word, never a smile in all those years. She'd sit in her chair in the Justice Room, talking to herself about her horses.

'No one came near the place, and that was fine by me. If ever they did, she'd drive them off with a shotgun and I'd help her. Just about the only thing we ever agreed on. We liked the place to ourselves. And then, about three years ago now, I found her sitting there in her chair staring out of the window, but her eyes weren't seeing. I closed them. I scattered her ashes on the croquet lawn where I had scattered Bengie.

'I had hopes after she died, high hopes. After all, I'd done everything for her, everything, hadn't I? She had no family, no friends. And I had a right to it. Didn't I have a right to something? So what does she do? She's got no one to leave it to, so she leaves it to everyone. She goes and leaves it all to the National Trust. All her life she hated people coming on to the place, and she knew I hated it too. She knew it! She did it to spite me. That's why next week, if she has her way, there'll be thousands of people trampling all over my place. And it is my place. Bengie promised me. I don't want them here. I won't have them! I won't allow it! I won't!' And he slapped the arm of his chair, slopping the tea on to his trousers. He sat glaring at me, his lips trembling. I didn't know what to say, so I said the first thing that came into my head.

'About the man I saw?' I asked him. 'The face in the attic window.'

'Just the plumber, I expect,' he said, 'come to put the tank in the attic. He's been finishing off for weeks.' He seemed to be struggling to compose himself. He went on. 'He'll be gone by now. He locks up, but I've got a secret key of my own. I expect you'll be wanting to see over the place, will you?' I thought he'd never ask.

I followed him down through the vegetable garden, a frail figure tottering ahead of me in the gloom, and talking as he went. 'I used to grow the best leeks in all Devon in this garden,' he said. 'And I dug the earliest potatoes too. Beautiful.'

We came at last into a dark courtyard behind the house. 'They don't like me going in,' he said. 'But I go where and when I please. Like I told you, it's my place.' The door opened and a light came on inside. 'You can find your own way round,' he said over his shoulder. 'I can't manage the stairs anymore. I'll wait for you in the Justice Room. That way.' And he stabbed a crooked finger in the direction of a closed door at the end of a dark corridor.

For half an hour maybe, I explored the house. I began in the huge kitchens and went down the stone steps into the vaulted cellars. In the dining-room I sat alone at the end of the long polished table gazing up at the portraits of my ancestors. None of them were smiling, and as I left the room I noticed that their eyes were following me out. I felt I was not at all welcome, that they were glad to see the back of me.

The drawing-room was sumptuous and grand – oriental carpets everywhere, veneered wood the colour of honey, landscape pictures on the walls and the most capacious armchairs I ever saw. I sank deep into one of them and stretched out my legs, my heels resting on the brass fenders. I had to imagine the log fire and the Wolfhounds at my feet, but it wasn't difficult.

After that I went upstairs and along the dark corridors. I looked in on each and every one of the bedrooms – I must have tried out a dozen beds. I was lying on the four-poster bed in the biggest bedroom, dreaming my grand illusions, when I heard footsteps above me. Someone was moving about up in the attic. I remembered the plumber, and thought no more of it.

It was some time before I could find my way back to the hallway where I had begun my tour. I opened the door at the end of the corridor and found the old man standing by the fireplace in a magnificent room with ornate plaster ceilings and chandeliers – by far the biggest and grandest room in the house.

'There you are,' he said. 'I was wondering where you'd got to. The Justice Room they used to call this. But there is no justice, is there, not in this world? There's only revenge. An eye for an eye. Bengie and me, we read poetry in here. We wrote a bit too. We'd play cards at that table over there. He shouldn't have treated me the way he did, he shouldn't have done it.' He leaned heavily on the back of a chair and looked around him. 'And that's where she sat in her chair looking out over the park. That's where I found her the day she died.' He was looking straight at me now, almost into me. 'I've been thinking – the soldier in the picture up there above the fire, he was a Bickford. He looks just like you, the spitting image, I'd say. Come to think of it, you and Bengie, you're just like he was when we came back here after the war. You seen all you want, have you?'

'The plumber's still here,' I said. 'I heard him up in the attic. I thought he'd gone.'

'Finishing off, always finishing off.' The old man turned away. 'I'll show you the croquet lawn if you like. Bengie always beat me at croquet. He cheated and I let him. He cheated at cards too, and I let him. But he cheated me once too often. They both did.'

We went outside and stood in front of the house on the croquet lawn. A mist was shrouding the valley and a white screecher owl flew low and silent over the fields. 'Not many of they owls left,' said Percy Glanville. 'You'd best be going. It's getting dark.'

And so I thanked him and left him standing on the lawn. I jumped the open ditch and walked down across the field towards the road. When I turned to wave, he was gone. I noticed too that the plumber's pick-up truck was gone. The last glint of red sun set fire to the attic window, the same window where I'd seen the face earlier that afternoon. I stopped only to collect a handful of red oak acorns to take home with me, souvenirs, so I wouldn't forget. Not that I'm likely to. My last sight of the house was from the bridge over the stream. It glowered at me through the mist and I was suddenly very relieved my family had decided to move to Vermont when they did. I was glad I hadn't been born there.

Has it been worth it, worth coming all this way just to see an old house? I think so. At least I know now where I come from and maybe, just maybe, that'll help to show me where I'm going – you never know. Then there's that old man and his story. You could write a whole book about that. I won't sleep tonight, that's for sure, thinking about him and that face in the window, and the plumber I heard but I never saw – unless he was the face in the window. I guess I'll never know.

I'm suddenly hungry. So I'll have a quick shower and grab a sandwich downstairs and a glass or two of their warm beer. I know I shouldn't, but like Oscar Wilde says, 'I can resist just about everything except temptation,' or something like that.

Then I'll have an early night. London tomorrow, then home. I'll be back in Vermont the day after. Two days Devon to Vermont – that's a whole lot quicker than it was for my ancestors.

A fire engine just went wailing by. A little toy of a thing compared to ours at home. I saw a house burning once back in Woodstock when I was a kid. It was a lovely starlit night, I remember, just like tonight. That fire was the most beautiful sight I ever saw and the most terrible too.

There was only one suspect and his trail was easy enough to follow. The plumber had seen a young man with a rucksack come walking up the drive towards the house. The landlord at the Nethercott Cross pub had served a young American a beer and listened to his tale of how he'd been visiting Nethercott House, searching for his roots. He'd even told him his name. And then at The George, Nathaniel Bickford had signed his name in the visitors' book; and everyone remembered the rainbow scarf. The farmer in the Land Rover who gave him a lift back to Hatherleigh remembered the stench of petrol on the young man. That was why he rang the police when it came on the television about the fire and about how the police were looking for a young American with a rucksack and wearing a rainbow-coloured scarf. Nathaniel Bickford had left so many clues behind him, it was almost as if he wanted to be caught.

The police tracked him down at Exeter St David's station. He was sitting on his rucksack waiting for the London train. Back at the police station, he told them everything just as it happened. He'd recorded it in his diary, he said. He handed it over willingly enough. He'd done nothing wrong. He'd help all he could. All he wanted was to get it over with, he said. He had a plane to catch. The detective read the diary carefully, making notes as he did so. When he'd finished he sucked on his pencil and looked across the table at Nat.

'There's just a few little things wrong with your story,' he said.

'What do you mean "wrong"?' said Nat, unable any longer to hide his impatience.

'This old man you mention, this Mr Glanville. He lived up there all right, in the cottage, like you say. We know that. But he doesn't any longer. He died two days ago in Barnstaple, in hospital. Heart failure. So it's hardly likely you were talking to him yesterday afternoon, is it? And that car, the Silver Ghost? We know about the car too. But it was never there yesterday, any more than Percy Glanville was. It was sold when the old lady died and that was three years ago. Made a fortune in the salerooms up in London. That's where they found the money to do the place up. But it broke his heart, poor old boy. Everyone around knows how much he loved that car. That was when he took to the drink.' Nat could feel his heart pounding. 'You're in deep trouble, young man, and what's worse, you're cocky with it, aren't you? You were so sure you were going to get away with it, you didn't even bother to wash your trousers, did you? You stink of petrol, you know that? What d'you think we are over here, stupid?' He waved the diary in Nat's face. 'And as for this. Fantasy! Storytime! But unfortunately for you there's a dead giveaway in it, right at the end, the bit about how you think a big fire's the most beautiful thing in the world. You wrote it, son. It's all in here.'

No matter how vociferously Nat insisted and argued, he could feel the incriminating evidence building up against him and around him like a wall. It was a nightmare he longed to wake from, but could not.

The police were convinced by now that they had enough evidence to hold Nathaniel Bickford on suspicion of arson. Then the report came in from the Fire Officer. The police expected it to confirm their suspicions. It did not. It said the fire had definitely not been started by petrol. The evidence was quite clear. It was started by a blow-torch left on in the attic. They had found it there, fused in the heat to the gas cylinder and the water tank. There was no question about it. The plumber must have left his blow-torch on and that was how the fire had begun. Probably an accident. There was certainly no evidence of arson. They had to let him go.

Nathaniel Bickford went home to Vermont the next day. Nearly thirty years later and he's never been back to England. As he always says when he tells the story, 'Once was quite enough.'

And on Spring Farm near Woodstock in Vermont, if you look in amongst the maple trees down by the Sugar House, you'll find a single young oak tree growing straight and strong, the only survivor of the acorns he brought back all those years ago from England. In the autumn its leaves are a flicker of red flame in amongst the glowing gold of the maples. Nathaniel Bickford never passes it without remembering.

Letter from Kalymnos

I was on holiday in Greece with my young family some years ago. We went diving off a boat. There was an Italian couple with us, young, newly married, happy. He went diving, and just never came up. We found his body later. It all happened on such a beautiful day.

August 24th, 1995

Dear Zo,

I've been trying to write to you for some time, but until now I haven't known what to say or how to say it. But I must write it now.

I expect you hate me after what I've done. I certainly couldn't blame you if you did. I just hope that, when you've read this letter, you'll understand why I did what I did, and then maybe you won't hate me quite so much.

All my life, the part of it I can remember, you've

been my best friend, ever since St John The Baptist Junior School, class one – Miss Parmenter's class. Who could forget Miss Parmenter, with her spectacles cut in half so that she could look daggers at you over the top? She caught me writing 'bum' on the back of my hand, and then she caught you giggling at it. I was always getting you into trouble. We noth had to write 'bum' a hundred times and take it to the head teacher so we wouldn't think it was funny any more. It didn't work, did it? Every class we were in, we always managed to sit next to each other, and you let me copy you whenever I needed to, which was often. Once we got to Pretoria Street Comp we still stuck together. We engineered it so that we both did French and English and archaeology right through to the sixth form. Silly really, because I was always hopeless at French. I still am.

And it wasn't just at school we stuck together. Home was wherever we ended up at four o'clock, your place or mine. When you had your glandular fever that time and you were in bed for a month, I came and read to you every day – Babar. I know those stories by heart. Whenever I think of elephants now, I think of you and glandular fever. Then, when Mum went into one of her depressions, you'd always be over at my place, and we'd clean up the house together to make her feel better; and when we'd finished, we'd lie on my bedroom floor and just talk. You'd tell me your secrets, and I'd tell you mine, most of them anyway. We were always together. And when Dad went off, I called you and you came round and I cried up against you. You told me we can't pick our parents, only our friends. I'd never thought of that. You told me that you'd never desert me, no matter what; and you kept your word. It was me that deserted you. But I didn't just desert you, did I? I betrayed you. I cheated you.

Boys. It was the only thing we really didn't see eye to eye about. I always thought you were so strange about them. You never looked at them. They just didn't seem to interest you, until Daniel. Not like me at all. I was never happy unless I had two or three of them chasing me. I knew you never liked the head hunter in me, but you never said anything. I don't remember you judging me, not once in all the time I've known you. I just thought the whole boy thing was a big game, and there weren't any rules. You made them up as you went along. You knew it wasn't like that, and you were right. I just didn't know it then, that's all.

More than anything, I want you to believe that what I did wasn't intentional. It just happened. Even that first day when you brought him into school – Daniel Duroy, your 'French exchange' – you were like the cat that got the cream. You adored him. I could see that. Everyone could. I couldn't see why. I mean, he was all right to look at, nothing special. But he was no Gérard Depardieu, was he? He was silent and unsmiling too. He scarcely seemed to notice I was there, and I wasn't used to that. You were happier for those three weeks than I'd ever seen you. You glowed, and I was so jealous. I think you knew I was too. It was because I missed you. You were always with him, wrapped up in him. You hardly noticed me all the time he was there. And once he'd gone home, you talked about nothing except Daniel and how wonderful he was, how kind, how sensitive, how intellectual, how unlike any other boy you'd ever met. We had first-year-sixth exams coming up and you didn't even swot. I'd never known you like it.

Then you got ill again with your glandular fever and you cried because the doctor wouldn't let you go back for your three weeks in France with Daniel. And what did you do? You asked if I would like to go in your place. Daniel liked me – he'd told you so. You'd go over and see him at Christmas instead maybe. That's how much you trusted me.

I didn't really want to go. I don't much like speaking French, and I wasn't sure how I would get on with Daniel. But it was three weeks away from school. And you'd told me his place was by the sea, you'd shown me the photos. Besides, anything would be better than hanging around home with Mum. She doesn't seem to mind whether I'm home or not, just so long as she has enough drink in the house. I had some money saved up. So I went.

The schools in France had already finished for the summer holidays. I don't think Daniel knew what to do with me at first. We hardly spoke, because I wouldn't try out my French; and, anyway, he seemed happy enough with silence. So I didn't make the effort.

He showed me round Concarneau. We saw the castle together. That was the last time I wrote to you, the day we went round the castle. We sent you a postcard of it, and we signed it together. I remember it because that was the moment I first knew I loved him. We were sitting on the quay in the sun, watching the yachts going in and out, dangling our legs over the side. I handed him your card to sign. There was a seagull eyeing us sideways. We laughed, and then we looked at each other and we loved each other. I can't explain it. I still can't.

After that I spoke English and he spoke French – we found it easier that way. We just talked and walked and talked and walked. His mother and father were never home, so when we weren't at the beach snorkelling and swimming, we were at home sitting on the lawn drinking cold apricot juice and talking. Not just talking; touching, kissing, loving. Not the groping and grappling I'd done before. He didn't know what he was doing any more than I did, but we managed. We managed together. Best of all was sleeping curled up into his back and waking to find him still there. I'd blow gently on the soft hair at the back of his neck until he woke. And we laughed, how we laughed. Not at anyone, not at each other; but because we were so happy, so completely right for each other.

Whenever his mother and father came home from work – I still don't know what they did, he had something to do with boats I think – we were always on our best behaviour again. We'd hold hands under the table and squeeze secret signals at one another. They're a bit prim and proper, and always busy-busy – the kitchen, the garden, the car. He was always washing the car. They have one of those cars that rises up on its wheels when it starts. It always made me giggle.

I'm telling you all this, Zo, not to make you angry, although I know it must, but because I want you to know how it was between us, how it was natural, right and good. After the first few heady days we began to talk a lot about you, and I told him often how we had nothing to feel guilty about. But no matter how hard I tried to reason it out and justify it so that I shouldn't feel guilty, I did, and so did Daniel.

I expect you began to wonder what was going on when you didn't hear any more after the card from Concarneau, but I just couldn't face telling you what had happened. When I didn't come back at the end of the three weeks, I knew you must have guessed. And by then I couldn't bring myself to tell you because I knew you knew, and I knew how much you'd be hating me.

I was due to catch the boat back home on the Sunday from Roscoff, but I just couldn't bear to leave him. I pretended to be ill, unfit to travel, stomach upset. Daniel's mother and father believed it. Why shouldn't they? As they said, English people often get stomach upsets in France. I phoned Mum and told her I'd be back as soon as I was better. She didn't seem bothered one way or the other. She never even asked me what it was I'd eaten or anything. From her voice I think she was drinking again. I really hate her when she's like that. I know it's not her fault, but I can't help myself. One thing's for sure. At least I'll never grow up like her.

During my 'illness', Daniel worked out a plan. It was simple. We'd go off together backpacking for as long as we could. We would go as far as his money would stretch. He'd done it before, so his parents wouldn't be worried about it. I told them Mum had said it was all right for me to stay on a while after I got better. They went along with it without a murmur. Too busy washing cars and cleaning kitchens to worry about it, I think. So we set off.

Three days and four nights later, we found ourselves here in Kalymnos, a little Greek island off the coast of Turkey. I sent a card to Mum, told her that I was better and that I'd be back before term began again. I knew she'd be mad at me for doing it, but I didn't care. I left no address, so we were on our own and no one knew where we were. We'd bought as much time as we needed. I did a bit of waitressing in the evenings in a café on the seashore. It paid the rent on the room we shared with a million mosquitoes. We swam and we made love, and we swam and we made love. I don't know why they call it seventh heaven, but if there is one, then we were there, for more than a month we were there, and it was wonderful.

It was Daniel's birthday and I knew he loved to go diving. There was a wonderful blue and white caique moored in the harbour, a diving-boat. It didn't cost much to go out for the day. It was my birthday present to him.

We went out on the most beautiful day I ever saw. The sea was a flat, calm, jade green over the sand, blue further out. There wasn't a whisper of wind, not a puff of cloud. We chugged out and dropped anchor in a bay along the coast. There were just a few flat-topped houses and a café beyond the beach. I lazed on the deck sunbathing while Daniel got himself all togged up. He flip-flopped around the deck, snorting into his breathing apparatus. Then he flapped his flipper at me and went over the side, a ten-metre dive, the instructor told me.

There was another couple on board the caique, Italians. He was called Enrico and she was called Gina. They were both beautiful. Everything was beautiful that day.

Daniel came up after half an hour or so, climbed on board and dripped all over me as he pulled his gear off. He looked like a god against the sun, my god. Olive skin, grey eyes, gorgeous. Laughing down at me, he told me I should try it, that it was so peaceful at the bottom of the sea, that you were really alone down there. I said I didn't want to be alone, that I wanted to be with him for ever. The instructor patted him on the shoulder to congratulate him, and then busied himself with the Italians as they prepared for their dive. That was when Daniel said he was thirsty and asked me if I wanted a drink. 'Coke,' I told him. The next thing I heard was a great splash, and when I stood up I saw he was swimming for the beach a hundred or so metres away. I remember wondering how he was going to manage to swim back all that way with a can of Coke in his hand. I watched him powering through the sea. He swam so well. He was made for it.

I dozed off while he was gone, not proper sleep, just thinking. I was thinking of you, Zo. I was always thinking of you and wondering how I was ever going to face you again. Then a shadow came over me. It was the instructor asking after Daniel. I told him where he had gone, and he frowned, shook his head and turned away from me. 'He shouldn't have,' he said. 'I told him. Every time you go down deep, stay out of the water for at least an hour after. I *told* him.'

He scanned the beach and the café with his binoculars. He called in the Italians and started up the engine. We were going looking for Daniel. I didn't see why he should be so worried. I wasn't. I knew Daniel swam like a fish.

The fishermen mending their nets had not seen him on the beach. He hadn't been seen in the café. We could see no one swimming out in the bay. One of the fishermen shook his head and told us where we should look. He would come and help. They would all come and help. He knew. They all knew, except me. I was still wondering what all the fuss was about. Daniel had clambered ashore somewhere and was making his way to the café. We just couldn't see him from where we were, that's all. But no one was searching the island, no one was looking on the shore. I watched from the deck of the caique. I kept telling the instructor they were all looking in the wrong place, that Daniel was ashore already. He said nothing. He didn't seem to want to look at me. They were all out in boats now, scouring the bay, leaning over and peering down into the sea.

The Italians were snorkelling in the shallows around one of the fishing boats when they found him.

I was there when they dragged him out and tried to revive him, but they never tried hard enough. They just gave up. I tried mouth to mouth, but they pulled me off him. Gina sat by me on the deck as we went back to port, her arm round me, and I looked at the dirty green tarpaulin that covered him, still hoping that it was all a nightmare, that any moment now the tarpaulin would move and Daniel would throw it off and sit up. I could see one of his feet. I willed his toes to move, but they never did.

Back at the harbour, the police were waiting with an open van. There were boxes of tomatoes in the back. They put him on a stretcher and laid him out in the van in the sun alongside the tomatoes. There were dozens of people crowding round, all wanting a look. I said I had to go with him in the van, but they wouldn't listen.

They wouldn't let me go with him. They took him away from me, and I never saw him again.

There were questions, lots of questions, about how it had happened, where he came from, where I came from. They took his passport and everything that was his, and left me alone in our room. That was when I really understood that he was dead for ever, gone from me, that I was quite alone in the world.

For two days now I've been here. I haven't moved from our room. Gina and Enrico are kind. They bring me food, grapes, and grilled fish and bread. But I don't want to eat and I can't seem to make them understand that. They sit with me, but we can't speak to one another. So they hug me long and hard, and cry, and then they leave me. And I'm alone again.

Daniel's mother and father will be here tomorrow, that's what the police told me. I suppose they'll take the body back to France. I don't want to see them. They'll blame me, and they'd be right to blame me. If I hadn't come instead of you, if I hadn't taken him away from you, if we hadn't been lovers, then Daniel would still be alive.

The light has gone out of my life, and I am alone in darkness. Daniel is gone. So I will go too. I will go down to the bay he drowned in. I will breathe in the sea water that he breathed in, and I'll go to be with Daniel wherever he is. If it's heaven, then we'll be there together. If it's not, if it's nowhere, if it's darkness, then I'd rather be in darkness with Daniel than alone and without him for the rest of my life.

Do you know that you're the only person in the world I'll miss? I think you're the only one who really knows me or cares. And look what I did to you. That's why I've written to you. Because I want you to forgive me. It's all I care about now.

I think it'll be easy. I hope so. I'll just walk into the sea and keep walking. I'm not frightened, Zo, really I'm not. You will forgive me, please?

Love,

Selina

The Beastman of Ballyloch

As a child I once had to be taken out of a pantomime performance of Beauty and the Beast. *I was simply terrified of the Beast. Ever since, the story has fascinated me. Then, many years later, I got to hear of an extraordinary, yet ordinary, invention, a mat made entirely of straw, which, if laid on the surface of a pond or a lake, sucks up the algae and lets the pond live and breath again. So I wrote my own* Beauty and the Beast. *Here it is.*

There was once an ogre so pitted and crumpled in his face, so twisted in his body, that no one could bear even to look at him. He was known in all the country around as the 'Beastman of Ballyloch'. He lived by himself on a small island in the middle of a great dark lake. Being left on his own as a small child, as he had been when his mother died, and shunned ever since by all humankind, he had never learned to speak as other men do, so that when he tried he sounded like a cawing, croaking crow, and no words came out.

Lonely though he was on his island, he was never completely alone, for with him lived all the wild things he loved so well – the squirrels, the otters, the herons and the moorhens. But of all the creatures that lived with him on the island, it was the swans he loved best. He mended their broken wings, untangled them from fishing twine and drove the marauding gulls away from their nests. For the swans, the island was a safe haven. They knew the ogre was not like the people who lived across the lake in the village of Ballyloch. He would not hunt them or steal their eggs, or throw sticks at them. To them, he was not at all hideous. He was their guardian and the kindest man that ever lived, a trusted friend.

He lived simply in the log cabin he had built for himself, under a roof he had thatched himself. Under the thatch it was cool enough in the summer months, and just so long as he kept the fire going, warm enough in the winter too. He grew all the corn he needed in his one-acre field, and all the vegetables he could want in the sheltered garden behind the log cabin. When the fish were rising of an evening in the great dark lake, then he would often go out in his boat

and catch himself a fine fat fish for his supper –
seatrout perhaps, or brown trout, or even better a
silver salmon fresh up from the sea. The ogre needed
to eat well, for he was half as big again as any man in
Ballyloch.

Much as the people of Ballyloch hated the sight of
the ogre, they needed him, for he was the best thatcher
for miles around and they knew it. He was also the
cheapest. All he asked in payment for a day's work was
a wheelbarrow load of peat for his fire. So whenever
there was a barn or a house to be rethatched, he would
set out across the lake in his boat, and he would always
be escorted by a flotilla of swans. The villagers would
see him coming, and the cry would go up. 'The
Beastman is coming! The Beastman is coming!' Many
of the children would be hustled away indoors as he
tied up his boat by the quayside, as he came limping up
the village street. Others, the older ones more often,
would laugh and jeer at him, throw stones at him even;
and then run off screaming up the alleyways. He did
not blame them. He had ears. He knew well enough
what they had all been told: 'Don't you ever go near
the Beastman. He's mad. He's bad. Don't ever set foot
on his island either. If you do he'll gobble you up.'

In spite of this, the ogre did his best to smile at
everyone. He would always wave cheerily; but not one

of them would ever wave back nor greet him kindly. The ogre endured all the averted eyes, all the wicked whisperings, all the children's taunts because he loved to be amongst his own, to hear the sound of human voices, to see the people at their work, the children at their play, to feel that he was once more a man amongst men. From high up on a rooftop, as he drove in his spars or combed his thatch, he could look down over the village and watch them all going about their lives. That was as close as he was ever going to get to them. He knew he could hope for nothing more. In all his life he had never once been invited into their houses, never once warmed himself at their hearths. He would do his day's thatching, wheel his barrowload of peat down to the quayside in the evening, load his boat and row back to his island across the great dark lake, his beloved swans swimming alongside.

It was a summer's day and there was a fresh run of seatrout in the lake. Dozens of fishing boats had come out from Ballyloch, and the sound of happy children rippled across the water. The ogre sat on the grassy bank of his island and watched them. He thought at first it was the sound of flying swans, their wings singing in the air; but then he saw her, a young woman in a straw hat. It was she who was singing. She was standing up in her boat and hauling in her line. Her boat was close to the island, closer to the shore than they usually came, much closer than all the other boats. How the ogre's heart soared as he listened. Nothing was ever as sweet as this.

There was a sudden shriek and a splash, and the boat was empty and rocking violently. The straw hat was floating on the water, but of the young woman there was no sign at all. The ogre did not stop even to take off his boots and his jacket. He dived straight into the icy water and swam out towards the boat. He saw her come up once, her hands clutching at the air before she sank again. She came up a second time, gasping for life, and was gone again almost at once. The ogre went down after her, caught her round the waist and brought her to the surface. He swam her back to the island and laid her down in the grass. She lay there, limp and lifeless, not a movement, not a breath. The ogre called and called to her, but she would not wake. He held his head in his hands and wept out loud.

'Why are you crying?' She was speaking! The ogre took his hands away. She was sitting up! 'You're the Beastman, aren't you?' she went on, shrinking from him. She looked around her. 'I'm on the island, aren't I? I shouldn't be here. I shouldn't be talking to you.' For a few moments she stared at him and said nothing. 'It must have been you that saved me. You pulled me out!' The ogre thought of speaking, but dared not. The sound of his croaking voice would only make him more fearsome, more repellent. The girl was suddenly smiling at him. 'You did, didn't you? You saved my life. But why? After all I did to you. When I was a child I used to throw stones at you, do you know that? I used to laugh at you. And now you've saved my life.'

The ogre had to speak, had to tell her none of that mattered, had to tell her how beautifully she sang. He tried, but of course all that came out was a crow's croak. 'All right,' she went on. 'Maybe you can't speak words, but you can speak. And you can hear me, can't you? My father – you know my father. He's the weaver. You thatched our house once when I was little, remember? He always told me you were bad. But you're not, are you? He said you were mad too, that you gobble up children for your tea. But you're not like that at all. I know from your eyes you're not. How can I ever thank you? I have nothing to give you. I am not rich. I know, I know. Shall I teach you how to speak words? Shall I? First I shall teach you my name – Miranda. Miranda. You will say it. You will.' The ogre took her small hands in his and wept again, but this time for sheer joy. 'And I'm going to tell everyone what you did, and they won't ever believe any more all the horrible things they've heard about you.' She shivered suddenly. 'I'm cold,' she said.

The ogre carried her into his cabin, set her down close to the fire, and wrapped her in his best blanket. He hung out her clothes to dry and gave her a bowl of piping hot leek and potato soup. Afterwards, warmed through inside and out, Miranda slept for a while; and the ogre sat and watched her, happier than he had been in his whole life.

By the time she woke, her clothes were dry again, and he rowed her back across the lake, towing her own boat behind them. She talked to him all the while, and that was when she told him of the smiling stranger with the pointed teeth who had just come to lodge in the village. 'No one knows where he comes from, but Father says he'll make us all rich. That's what everyone says. He may too, but I don't think so. There's something shifty about him. He smiles too much. Father says he'd make me a good husband. I tell you, I'd rather marry a billygoat. Him and his magic Stardust! "What do you most want in all the world?" he says. Well, of course, everyone says the same thing, don't they? "We want to be rich."'

The ogre had stopped rowing, leaving the boat drifting towards the quay. 'Stardust. Stardust.' The word rang in his head like a warning bell. '"All you have to do is sprinkle my Stardust on your cornfields," says the smiling stranger,' she went on, '"and your corn will grow faster in a week than in a whole year. Sprinkle Stardust on the lake and before the week's out you'll be catching fish as big as whales." All we have to do is buy his silly Stardust.'

At this the ogre became suddenly very agitated, croaking and cawing as if wracked inside by some terrible pain. She tried to understand him. She tried to calm him. She wasn't to know the terrible story echoing now in his head, how his mother had told him on her deathbed of the smiling stranger with the pointed teeth who had come to their house just before he was born, and asked her exactly the same question: 'What do you most want in all the world?' 'A boy child who will grow big and strong,' she had said. And she'd paid him all her life savings. 'Sprinkle this magic Stardust on your supper tonight, and you shall have your wish,' the smiling stranger had said, and he'd taken the money and ridden away on his fine horse. Only weeks later his mother had given birth to a baby boy, bigger and stronger than any man child ever born, but ugly as sin and as misshapen as it is possible to be, and with a voice that croaked like a crow.

The ogre reached forward and clasped Miranda's hands, striving all he could to say the words to warn her, but they would not come. 'Don't worry,' she told him. 'I shall come back. I promised to teach you to speak, didn't I? And I shall. I will come tomorrow. Tomorrow I shall teach you my name. I promise. I promise.'

As the boat touched the quay she leapt out and ran away. Suddenly she stopped and turned to him, her hand on her head. 'My straw hat. I think I've lost my straw hat. But why am I complaining about a silly hat when I have my life? Thank you, thank you for my life.' And the ogre watched her go, his heart crying out after her, until he could see her no more in the gathering dusk.

That evening, as the ogre sat alone and wretched in his log cabin, the people of Ballyloch gathered in their hall to hear the smiling stranger with the pointed teeth tell them how everyone of them could be ten, twenty times as rich, a hundred times as rich inside a week. 'Sprinkle this magic Stardust,' he declared, 'and you will harvest gold.' They all listened in silence, and wondered and believed; but Miranda was not there to hear it.

Nothing ever happened in Ballyloch without the whole world knowing it. She had been seen coming back from the island with the ogre. As soon as she got home her father had sent her to her room and locked her in. Through the door she had tried to tell him how the ogre had rescued her from drowning, how he was kind and gentle and not at all as everyone said he was. She begged him to let her go back to the island the next day so that she could fulfil her promise and teach him how to speak.

'Never,' thundered her father. 'Promise me you will never go back there, or you will stay in your room till you do, d'you hear me?' But Miranda would promise no such thing.

So she was not there to protest when the villagers bought their sacks of Stardust from the smiling stranger with the pointed teeth. But she *was* watching from her window the next morning as they sprinkled their Stardust all over their cornfields, and out on to the great dark lake. From his island the ogre saw it too, and hung his head in despair. Somehow he had to warn Miranda when she came. Somehow he had to make her understand. All day he sat and watched and waited for her boat, but no boat came anywhere near his island. By nightfall Miranda had still not come.

All night long he sat there, all the next day, all the next week. Still she did not come and she did not come. On the seventh day, cries of delight echoed across the water as the villagers hauled gigantic fish out of the lake, fish so huge they could scarcely drag them into their boats. And the ogre could see clearly enough from the island that the corn in the fields was already twice the height it had been the week before. On the seventh night the ogre sat by the lakeside and listened to the sound of revelry wafting over the still dark water. He knew it for certain now. There was no hope. She would never come back to him. Those eyes of hers which had promised so much would, like the smiling stranger's magic Stardust, bring nothing but pain.

Distant thunder sounded through the mountains, heralding a storm; but still the ogre did not seek the shelter of his cabin. When the lightning crackled and crashed overhead, he did not move. He wished only that it would strike him dead. When the cold rain lashed down on him and the wind howled across the lake and chilled him to the bone, he sat where he was and prayed he would freeze to death so that he would not have to face the morning.

Morning came though, and he found himself numb all over, but still alive. The storm had passed by. The morning sun broke through the mist and warmed him. Beside him the swans slept, heads tucked under their wings. That was when the ogre first heard the wailing from across the water. Everyone in the village was out in the streets and gazing up at their houses. Every roof in the village had been ripped off and the thatch strewn about the streets. Out in the cornfields there was no corn left standing. Everywhere the people stood dazed and weeping. Many of them were down at the water's edge and looking out over the lake in stunned horror.

Only then did the ogre notice it himself. The lake was no longer dark. It was green, an unnatural green such as he had never seen before. He knelt down by the lakeside and ran his hand through the water. It wasn't the water that was green. It was covered on the surface by a thick layer of slime. Further out, a moorhen bobbed about in it, green all over. She tried to take off, tried to fly, but could not. An otter ran along the shore, not black and glistening as he usually was, but entirely green from head to tail. And fish lay dead in the water, on the shore, everywhere the ogre looked. And his swans, his beloved swans, were gliding through it, dipping their long and lovely necks. He shouted at them to come back, but it was too late. As they washed and preened themselves, every one of them was turning green. Already some of them were choking. He ran to the end of the island to see if the lake was green all around. It was, as far as the eye could see. A solitary duck quacked from in amongst the reeds. She tried to fly, but her feathers were matted and heavy with slime. The ogre knew she was never going to fly again.

As he watched her struggling in vain to clean

herself, the ogre noticed Miranda's straw hat floating in amongst the reeds, and around it the only clear dark water in the entire lake. He waded out and picked it up. One look underneath the dripping hat and his heart surged with sudden hope. All his years of thatching told him it was possible. Miranda's hat proved it. But the lake was dying all around him. Soon not a fish would be left alive; and he knew that unless he could save them in time, all his beloved swans would die too.

He rowed out over the green lake, and as he rowed he saw dead fish floating all around him, bloated on the water. A drowned cormorant drifted by and a heron aarked in terror from the shore, flapping his great wings in a frantic effort to rid himself of the cloying green cloak that would not let him fly. For once the people of Ballyloch paid him little attention as the ogre walked amongst them. They were too busy bemoaning their disaster.

'We brought it on ourselves,' one was saying. 'How were we to know?' said another. 'The stranger promised we'd be rich, and look what ruin he has brought on us instead.' 'We will have no corn to harvest. There will be no fish to catch. We will all starve, all of us.' 'What have we done to deserve this? What have we done?'

The ogre left them and hurried straight to the

weaver's house. From her window, Miranda saw him coming and called down to him. 'I tried to come, I tried, but Father forbad me from ever seeing you again. He made me promise I would never go to the island, and when I refused, he shut me in here. I have not been allowed out of my room for a week. And look what has happened in that week. It was the stranger's magic Stardust that did this, I know it was.'

The ogre waved her straw hat in the air, and tried all he could to tell her what he had discovered, but she could make no sense of all his frantic cawing and croaking. 'Just come up and let me out, and then you can tell me. But hurry, hurry, before Father comes back.' The ogre let himself in at the front door and climbed the stairs to Miranda's room. Once the door was unlocked, she took him by the hand and they ran out into the weaving shed where they could be alone and unseen. There, with the roof open to the skies, and the thatch strewn all around their feet, the ogre showed her the straw hat and explained to her as best he could what had to be done to save the lake, and the fish, and the swans, and the people of Ballyloch too. When he had finished, she reached up and touched his face tenderly. 'You are no Beastman,' she said. 'You are the *Bestman*, the best man in Ballyloch, the best man in all the world.'

When the people heard the churchbell ringing out, they gathered in the village, believing it was the mayor who had called them together. But the mayor was as puzzled as everyone else when out of the church came Miranda, her straw hat in her hand, and looming behind her the huge form of the Beastman of Ballyloch. Her father was spluttering in his fury, but before he could find the words to protest, Miranda began:

'The fish cannot breathe and the birds cannot fly,' she said. 'The lake is poisoned. If it cannot be saved, then we, too, will die with it. Like the otters, like the herons, we cannot live without our fish.'

'Why is the Beastman here?' cried her father, pushing though the crowd. 'I told you to keep away from him.'

'Get him away. We don't want him near the children,' said the mayor. 'Send him back to his island. We don't need him.'

'And who will thatch our roofs if he does not?' Miranda was angry now, angrier than she had ever been, and they heard it in her voice. No one could answer her. No one dared answer her, not even her father. She spoke only softly, but everyone listened. 'I'm telling you, we need him for more than thatching, too. He has come to save the lake, and he is the only one among us who can. He can't tell you how, because he can't speak as we do. So, for now, I shall speak for him.'

She held up her straw hat for everyone to see. 'Only a few days ago, this man, this ogre, this mad, bad Beastman, saved me from drowning. He didn't gobble me up, he saved my life. I was wearing this hat when I fell in and I thought it was lost. He found it this morning in the lake, and he saw that all around it the water was clear. Look underneath, and you will see how it soaks up the green slime that is choking the life out of our lake. His idea is that we should weave, all of us together, a huge straw carpet and lay it out on the lake. We shall weave it with flax – Father has enough flax in his weaving sheds to do it. It can be done. It must be done. We have all the straw we need, all the corn broken by the storm, all the thatch lying loose in the streets. Once the carpet is made, we shall tow it out and leave it on the lake to soak up the green slime.'

They stood, mouths agape. No one spoke a word. 'We must have the carpet on the lake by nightfall,' Miranda went on. 'We may be too late already to save all the fish, and all the birds; but we may still save most of them if we hurry. We may even save ourselves.'

No one argued, not even her father. Soon every man, woman and child was out gathering the strewn thatch and the battered corn, and spreading it out to be woven into a great straw carpet. All day they toiled, Miranda and the ogre amongst them. For the very first time in his life the ogre felt the warmth of their smiles. No one stopped for a moment, not for food, not for drink. They worked till their backs ached, till their hands were raw, until the carpet of straw was woven together at last. When they had finished, it stretched along the lakeside from one end of the village to the other. At dusk, towed by twenty fishing boats, they hauled it out on to the lake and left it floating there. Neither the ogre nor Miranda nor anyone could do any more. Now the straw had to be left to work its magic. How the people of Ballyloch prayed that night that the straw magic would be stronger than the Stardust magic of the smiling stranger. How they prayed that their lake could be saved.

When the ogre rowed home to his island that night, Miranda was with him. Time and again they stopped to scoop half-drowned birds from the slime, so that by the time they reached the island, the bottom of the boat was filled with them, all struggling for life. Once inside his cabin, they cleaned them off as best they could with straw wisps and clean water, and then they set about bringing in all the surviving swans they could find. They, too, had to be cleaned off and washed down, until their feathers were white again and gleaming in the firelight.

All night, as they worked together, Miranda was teaching him. Tired as he was, he was determined to be able to say at least one word by morning. Over and over again he practised 'Miranda'; and by morning he could say 'Manda', which, she said, was as good, if not better, than Miranda anyway. It was a start. There would be many more nights, she said, and many more words.

Both were dreading the coming of dawn, for the glow of love was over them, and like all lovers they wanted time to stand still. But in the back of their minds, too, was the awful fear that the green slime would still be there in the morning, that the straw carpet might have failed them. They fell asleep by the fire, the swans all around them.

They were woken by the sound of cheering, and ran outside. Every boat in the village, it seemed, was heading towards the island. And the lake was dark once more, and dancing with the early morning sun. The straw magic had worked! There were still some patches of green close to the shore, but they were few and far between. There would be enough clear water now for the fish to breathe, for the birds to wash themselves clean. The people of Ballyloch leapt out on to the grassy bank, hoisted the ogre and Miranda on to their shoulders and carried them off in triumph around the island. Above them flew the swans, their wings singing in the air.

Set down at last on their feet again, Miranda kissed away in one minute all the sadness the ogre had stored up inside him all his life. 'This is my man,' she declared joyously. 'This is the *Bestman* of Ballyloch.' And there was not a soul there who disagreed. 'And who,' she asked him, 'who is the best girl in Ballyloch?'

'Manda,' said the Bestman of Ballyloch. 'Manda. Manda.'

By the time they married a few months later, he could say the name of everyone who lived in Ballyloch, and could tell Miranda what every bird he saw was called, and every animal too come to that. After that he very soon learnt to talk well enough to make himself understood. Of course his work was more in demand than ever after the storm damage. Now wherever he went, he was invited in to eat at their tables and to warm himself at their hearths.

He was mending the roof on the weaving shed when Miranda's father came in carrying over his arm the biggest and most beautiful jacket he had ever made.

'For you,' he said. 'This is to ask your pardon, and to

thank you for saving my daughter, for saving all of us.' The ogre tried it on and it fitted perfectly. 'You do not need to live out on your island any more,' said Miranda's father. 'Come and live with us in the village. You are one of us now.'

'It is kind of you, and this jacket is fit for a prince,' said the ogre. 'But Manda and I, we must stay with our swans.'

It was some time later that their first child was born out on the island, a girl child; and she was as healthy and as beautiful as it is possible to be. They were sitting by the fire one evening, the child sleeping in the cradle beside them. The ogre was silent with his own thoughts, thoughts Miranda found she could often guess at just by looking at him. 'She does not know it yet,' he said. 'But when she grows up, she will know I am ugly.'

'You are not ugly,' cried Miranda. 'You are as beautiful as your daughter is beautiful, as beautiful as your swans are beautiful. Do you think I would look twice at some smooth-faced Prince Charming? You're my man, my Bestman, and don't you forget it. I love you, every bulbous bump of you, every craggy crease of you, you great oaf! Now, off with you and catch my supper.'

'Salmon or trout?'

'Trout tonight,' she said. 'I feel like a nice fat brown trout.'

'Well, you don't look like one,' he replied, and he was gone out of the door before she could find anything to throw at him.

In Ancient Time

William Blake once asked the question: 'And did those feet in ancient time, Walk upon England's mountains green?' Maybe, just maybe . . .

England. First Century AD.

When I was young we heard it often, all of us in the village did, but whenever the old man began his story again, we listened rapt all the same. He was blind in his last years, but every time he told the story his eyes blazed as if he was seeing it happen in front of him as he spoke. He finished always with the same words. 'See! He's here! He's here with us now.' And he would point over our heads into the smoky darkness beyond the fire. Time and again I would find myself turning round to look, and I wasn't the only one. Like the wind through the trees before the rain, we always knew when the story was coming. He would wait for a silence around the fire, lean forward warming his hands, and begin.

'In ancient time before any of you were even born, I was a young man. No cursed Roman soldier had yet set foot in this land of ours. We were not then a beaten people. We were wild perhaps, quarrelsome certainly, but we were our own people.

'My mother died in giving birth to me, and my beloved father fed me, taught me and protected me. Wherever I went I walked in his steps. He was a god to me. Then one day, whilst I was still only a small boy, he went off hunting into the forest with his brother, my uncle, and did not return. He had been attacked by a bear and taken off. Not a bone was ever found of him. That was what they told me. My uncle, who had no children of his own, took me in, and at once treated me as his slave. I gathered his firewood for him. I set his traps. I skinned his deer. I ground his corn. He was a giant of a man with arms like treetrunks, and the neck of a bull, and he had a raging temper too. It was not until I was nearly a man myself that I at last found the courage to stand up to him, to protest at how I had been used all these years.

'"You whining wretch," he cried. "Have I not fed you, clothed you, kept you warm through the winters?" And in his fury he took a great staff and beat me to the ground. Blow upon blow he rained down on me. I curled up like a hedgehog to protect myself. I would have lain there cowering in the dirt. But as he struck me he began to shout at me, a vicious curse with each blow, with each kick. And then after the curses came these terrible words: "I killed your miserable father, kicked him to death in the woods till there was no breath left in him. Like you, he too turned on me, and enraged me. Like this I killed him, and this, and this, and then left him to the bears and the wolves. So I will leave you. Your blood shall join his blood."

'Vengeance gave me all the strength I needed. With a scream of anger, I rose up and tore the staff from his grasp. I struck him about the body, about the head until he fell on his knees and begged me to stop, but I did not stop until he was stretched out lifeless at my feet. I ran then, stumbling into the forest, knowing full well that after what I had done I would never see my childhood friends again, nor ever return to my village, that I would wander an outcast for ever, alone all my life, a killer man, a cursed man.

'I went west always towards the setting sun, and after many weeks, found myself high on a windswept moor, in amongst the sacred mounds where great chieftains lie buried, and the sea about me on both sides. It was a darkening winter's evening. The howling cold bit into my bones and froze my spirits. For some days I had had little or nothing to eat, and no shelter either. I was a lost man, filled with remorse at my terrible crime, with nowhere to lay my head, no one to comfort me. I saw no hope, no end to my suffering. I wandered wailing in my misery through the high bracken that whipped me about the face and the grasping gorse that ripped at my clothes and at my flesh beneath, until at last I came to the edge of a towering cliff with the sea surging far below me. Here, I thought, here I shall end my life for it is not worth the living. I would be resolute. I would be brave. I stepped forward, but found that I could not, that my legs would simply not obey me. I felt a sudden hand on my shoulder.

'"Friend," said a voice. I turned.

'He was a man still young, but older than I was, taller too and with a darker skin. He had eyes that looked into my very soul. "Come," he said and, putting his arm round my shoulders, he led me away from the cliff edge. I found I had neither the will nor the power to resist him.

'"You need food. You need warmth. You shall stay with my uncle and me," he said. "We live close by. It's not much of a place to live, but it is out of the rain, out of the mists. We have a warming fire and there'll be food enough and plenty for another one. Come."

'So they took me in. He called himself Jesus, Jesus of Nazareth, and his old uncle I came to know as Joseph of

Arimathea. I had heard of neither place. They were travellers, they told me, who had come from an eastern land across the sea. They had come as far west as they could and were working a tin mine nearby. It would be hard work, they said, but they could always do with help, with another strong back, another pair of hands. So, for a winter, a spring and a summer, the three of us lived together, and side by side hammered and hewed in the tin mine. My spirits were restored and my strength too. I lacked for nothing, food, water, shelter, and most welcome of all, human companionship.

'There was often silence between us, but it was the silence of friends at ease with one another. Both seemed often deep in meditation and prayer, and more and more I found myself drawn too into their life of contemplation. When they did talk they spoke of such wonders, such places and people as I could never have imagined. From them I first heard of the Romans, who already ruled their country and much of the rest of the world too it seemed. It was a rare and wonderful thing, they said, to come to a place where the Romans did not rule. They had been as far east as they had west on a great voyage of discovery. They talked of mountains as high as the sky itself, of great temples high in the mountains of the east, of wise men and visionaries they had encountered in their travels; but

most often they told me of their God, a god so power-
ful that he would one day prove stronger than even
the mighty Romans themselves, and yet at the same
time he was a merciful god who loved us, and forgave
us, when we did wrong.

'I listened in wonder to all of this – Jesus was a man
I had to listen to, I wanted to listen to – and in time I
began to ask questions for there was much I did not
understand. "Who is this god you speak of? Where is
he? Where will I find him?"

'"He is in me," Jesus replied. "He is in my uncle
Joseph, and he is in you too. He is in all of us, if we
want him to be." This Jesus could seem somewhat
obtuse sometimes. I was none the wiser. In all this time
neither Jesus nor his uncle Joseph ever asked why I
had come there or how it was that I had been found in
so wretched a state, ready even to kill myself.

'We were sitting silent around the fire one autumn
evening. I was filled with remorse, as I always was
when contemplating my dreadful crime. I looked up
and found them both watching me. There was no accu-
sation in their eyes, only a tenderness, an
understanding that moved me at last to speak out and
tell them my story. When I had done, Jesus reached out
and put his hand on mine.

'"Go home where you belong," he said. "Your uncle

lives. I tell you he is not dead." He spoke with such certainty. "We will go together, for the time has come when we too must go home where we belong. We have wandered long enough in this wilderness. I have God's work to do, and I must wait no longer."

'So early one morning with the autumn mists still shrouding the valleys we set off together. The closer we came to my village the more I worried how I might be received, and the more I began to doubt Jesus' assurances that I would find my uncle was still alive. We parted by the river below the village, in the shadow of the great alder trees where the salmon lie low in the pools. I was fearful, and reluctant to leave my companions. I urged them to accompany me into my village. "Go on alone, friend," Jesus whispered as he embraced me. "All shall be well."

'"If ever you need us, come to Palestine. You will find us easily enough," said Joseph. And they left me to find my own way.

'It was as Jesus had said. My uncle was indeed alive. More than that, he was a changed man, utterly changed. He fell on his knees begging me for forgiveness before the whole village. I could see at once that he meant it, that all the fury and cruelty had gone out of him. I forgave him readily, knowing only too well what agony of remorse he had been through. There was great feasting and rejoicing that night, for I had long been supposed dead.

'But despite all my uncle's kindnesses to me – he treated me with such affection after my return, like a long lost son – I found myself restless, no longer content to stay all my life in my village. I longed to go to Palestine to be again with Jesus and Joseph. So after only three summers at home I set off on my own voyage of discovery. I travelled over the sea into Gaul, to Rome itself, then by ship again to Egypt and across the desert at last to Palestine. The closer I came the more I heard of Jesus of Nazareth, how his words touched the hearts of the people, of the poor and the downtrodden, how he had given hope where there was none. Some said he made miracles. Some were calling him the Messiah. Some said he would set them free and drive the Romans from their soil for ever. He was on his way to Jerusalem, they said.

'So I went at once to Jerusalem to meet him. There were very few people about. I asked after him in the market place. They just laughed at me and told me I had better hurry. "Why?" I asked.

'"Why do you think there's hardly anyone here in the market? Always the same when they crucify someone – half the city goes to watch – ruins our trade. It's all his fault, that Jesus of Nazareth. It's him they're crucifying, him and a couple of thieves."

'"Where?" I could scarcely find my voice.

'"Golgotha," they told me and pointed up the hill. "Outside the city walls. Just follow the crowd."

'So I did. I joined the surge of the crowd as they packed the narrow streets, pushing and jostling my way through until at last I found him. He was staggering under the weight of his cross, Roman guards whipping him on like a donkey as he went. Someone had pressed a cruel crown of thorns on to his head and his face was running with blood.

'Our eyes met, and he knew me at once. He smiled through his pain. "All shall be well, friend," he said.

'Swept along by the crowd, I followed. I was there when they nailed him to his cross and raised him high. Those same accursed Romans that now infest every corner of our land stood there and mocked him in his agony. But Jesus shouted no curses at them. He simply said: "Father forgive them. Father forgive them."

'He took almost all day to die. As I watched huddled under my cloak, my eyes filled with tears of anger, tears of grief, I felt a hand on my shoulder. "Come, friend, we have seen enough. Come away." It was his uncle Joseph, Joseph of Arimathea. We left Jerusalem that same morning. It was not safe to stay. Every one of Jesus' friends was being sought out and hunted down. In fear of our lives we moved from village to village, travelling only by night, and hiding by day.

'One day, hiding out in the dark depths of a mountain cave, he showed me the cup for the first time. "This cup," he told me, "is the very cup Jesus drank from at the last supper he ate with his friends. I shall hide it somewhere where it will be safe, safe for ever."

'Joseph was very tired and frail by now, and I knew we could not keep on running for much longer. "Let's go home, Joseph," I said. "Let's go back to my land, my village. There are no Romans there. We'll be safe. The cup will be safe." He was too exhausted to argue.

'The journey was long and arduous, so it was nearly winter before we came home at last. And for one short autumn we lived here together, Joseph and I, in my uncle's house. Never a day went by that we did not speak of Jesus. We drank from his cup every evening at supper – it was one way we could feel close to him. To both of us the world seemed such an empty place without him. Sometimes he liked to walk up the tor at Glastonbury to watch the sunset. He found the climb hard, and often had to lean heavily on his staff. We were up there at the top one evening as the world went dark around us.

'"Bury me here on this hill, friend," he said, "with

Jesus' cup beside me. He is here with us now. Can you feel him?" And I could. I could.

'When the time came, I did as he had asked me. I laid him deep in the earth of Glastonbury Tor, set the cup from the last supper in his hands and filled his grave. As I walked away, I drove his staff into the ground and left it there.

'I did not go back until the snows came. At the very place I had left his staff there now grew a great hawthorn tree, covered in white blossom. It is still there to this day. Blind as I am, I can see it now, as I can see Jesus. See! He is here! He is with us now.'

The old man died many long years ago, and I myself am now as old as he was. The Romans are still here, but one day they will be gone and we shall be our own people again. The hawthorn tree still blossoms on Glastonbury Tor in the depths of every winter and, rest assured, it always will. Now it is I who sit by the fire and tell the old man's story to the young ones. Each time I tell it I feel as if I am passing on something precious, more precious even than the cup that still lies buried somewhere on Glastonbury Tor.

Michael Morpurgo

Kensuke's Kingdom

Shortlisted for the Whitbread Children's Book Award.

I heard the wind above me in the sails. I remember thinking, this is silly, you haven't got your safety harness on, you haven't got your lifejacket on. You shouldn't be doing this. Then the boat veered violently and I was thrown sideways. I had no time to grab the guard-rail. I was in the cold of the sea before I could even open my mouth to scream.

Washed up on an island in the Pacific, Michael struggles to survive on his own. He can't find food, he can't find water. In the end, he curls up to die. When he wakes there is a plate beside him of fish, of fruit, and a bowl of fresh water. He is not alone . . .

'excellent . . . Beautifully written adventure story.'
The *Observer*

'dreamy . . . this is a thoughtful, elegiac story; the author's many fans will not be disappointed.'
The *Independent*

'Michael Morpurgo's latest novel bursts into life when the action hits the island and Michael starts fending for himself . . . an absorbing read.'
The *Daily Telegraph*

'The writing is in a class of its own. It is not just the presence of the Japanese soldier which brings this island to life. It is the author's imagination and careful attention to detail . . . Hugely satisfying.'
Carousel

Michael Morpurgo

War Horse

Runner-up for the Whitbread Children's Book Award.

In England, Albert is growing up on a Devon farm with his young horse Joey. In Germany, Friedrich works in his butcher's shop. In France, Emilie and her brothers play in their orchard. But the clouds of war are on the horizon and great armies are gathering their strength. Soon they will all be drawn into the nightmare of battle.

This is the story of Joey and the people whose lives he touches, as they struggle for survival in the blasted wilderness of the Western Front.

'. . . very moving, sparely and beautifully written and well researched . . . Michael Morpurgo shows us both the heroism and tragic futility of war.'
Jilly Cooper, *Times Literary Supplement*

Michael Morpurgo

Why The Whales Came

'You keep away from the Birdman,' warned Gracie's father. 'Keep well clear of him, you hear me now?'

But Gracie and her friend Daniel discover that the Birdman isn't mad or dangerous as everyone says. Yet he does warn them to stay away from the abandoned Samson Island – he says it's cursed. And when the children are stranded on Samson by fog, Gracie returns home to learn of a tragic death. Could the Birdman be right?

'a wonderful story . . .'
School Librarian

'excellent . . .'
The *Observer*

Why the Whales Came has been made into a major feature film starring Helen Mirren and Paul Scofield.